Dear parents, caregivers, and educators:

If you want to get your child excited about reading, you've come to the right place! Ready-to-Read *GRAPHICS* is the perfect launchpad for emerging graphic novel readers.

All Ready-to-Read *GRAPHICS* books include the following:

- ★ A how-to guide to reading graphic novels for first-time readers
- ★ Easy-to-follow panels to support reading comprehension
- ★ Accessible vocabulary to build your child's reading confidence
- ★ Compelling stories that star your child's favorite characters
- ★ Fresh, engaging illustrations that provide context and promote visual literacy

Wherever your child may be on their reading journey, Ready-to-Read *GRAPHICS* will make them giggle, gasp, and want to keep reading more.

Blast off on this starry adventure . . . a universe of graphic novel reading awaits!

Provided by:
Virginia Beach Library Foundation
and
Friends of the Virginia Beach Public Library

Worm and Caterpillar Are Friends

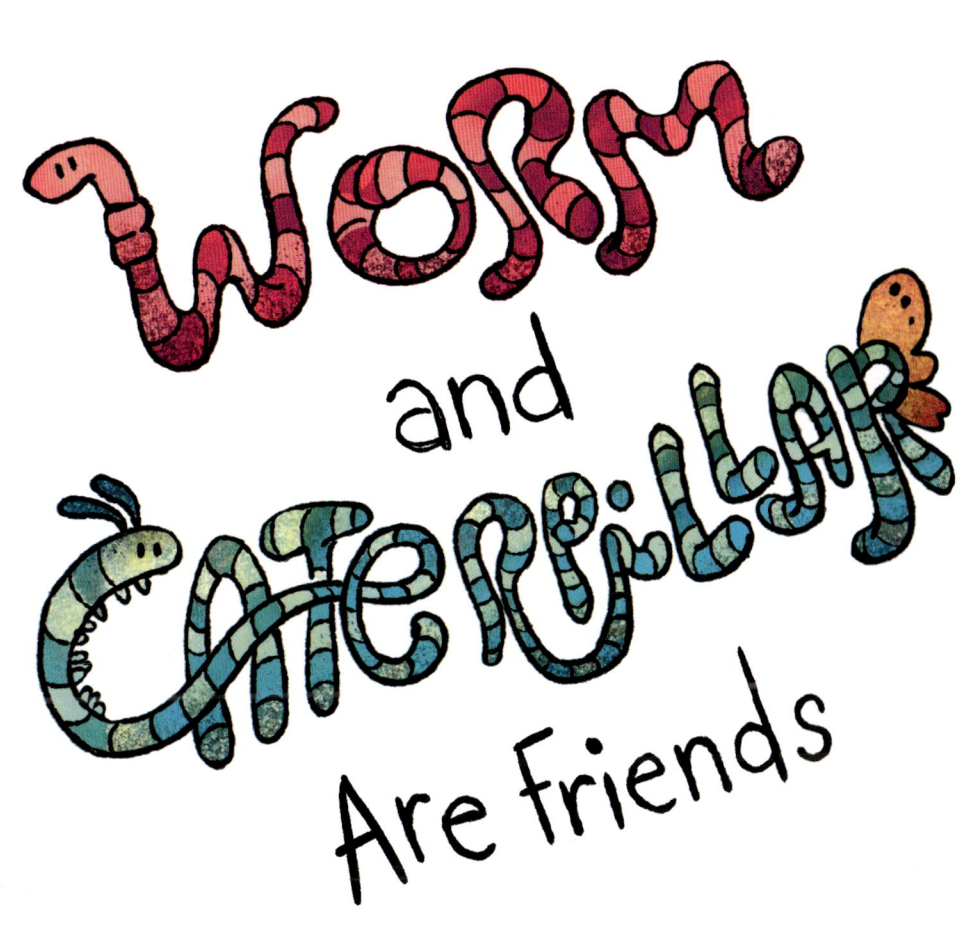

For my forever friend, Billy

SIMON SPOTLIGHT
An imprint of Simon & Schuster Children's Publishing Division
1230 Avenue of the Americas, New York, New York 10020
This Simon Spotlight edition January 2023
Text and illustrations copyright © 2023 Kaz Windness
All rights reserved, including the right of reproduction in whole or in part in any form.
SIMON SPOTLIGHT, READY-TO-READ GRAPHICS, and colophon are registered trademarks of Simon & Schuster, Inc.
For more information about special discounts for bulk purchases, please contact Simon & Schuster Special Sales at 1-866-506-1949 or business@simonandschuster.com.
The Simon & Schuster Speakers Bureau can bring authors to your live event. For more information or to book an event contact the Simon & Schuster Speakers Bureau at 1-866-248-3049 or visit our website at www.simonspeakers.com.
Manufactured in China 1022 SCP
2 4 6 8 10 9 7 5 3 1
This book has been cataloged with the Library of Congress.
ISBN 978-1-6659-2001-8 (hc)
ISBN 978-1-6659-2000-1 (pbk)
ISBN 978-1-6659-2002-5 (ebook)

Worm and Caterpillar Are Friends

Written and Illustrated by
Kaz Windness

Ready-to-Read *GRAPHICS*

Simon Spotlight
New York London Toronto Sydney New Delhi

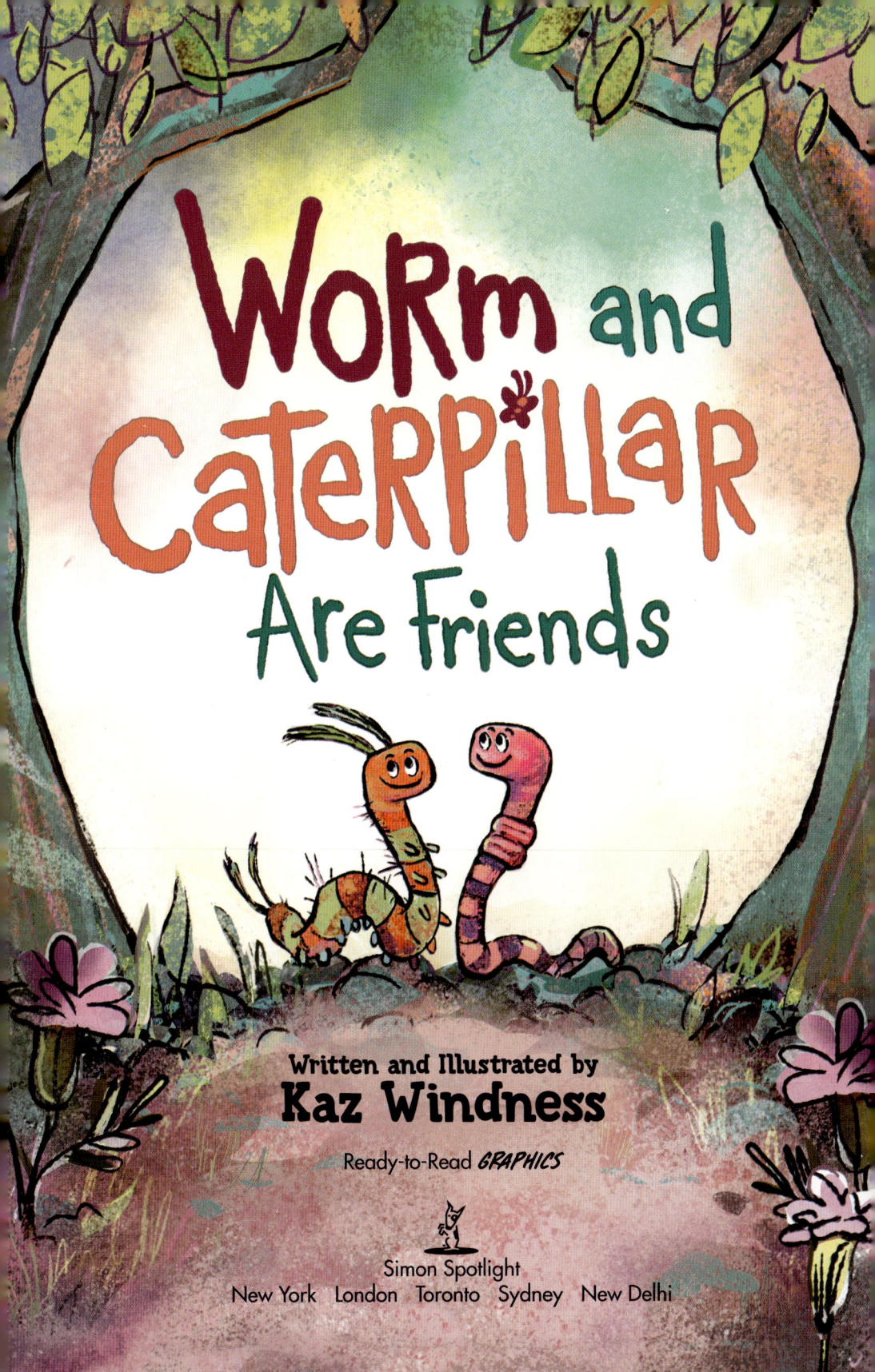

How to Read This Book

Worm and Caterpillar are here to give you some tips on reading this book.

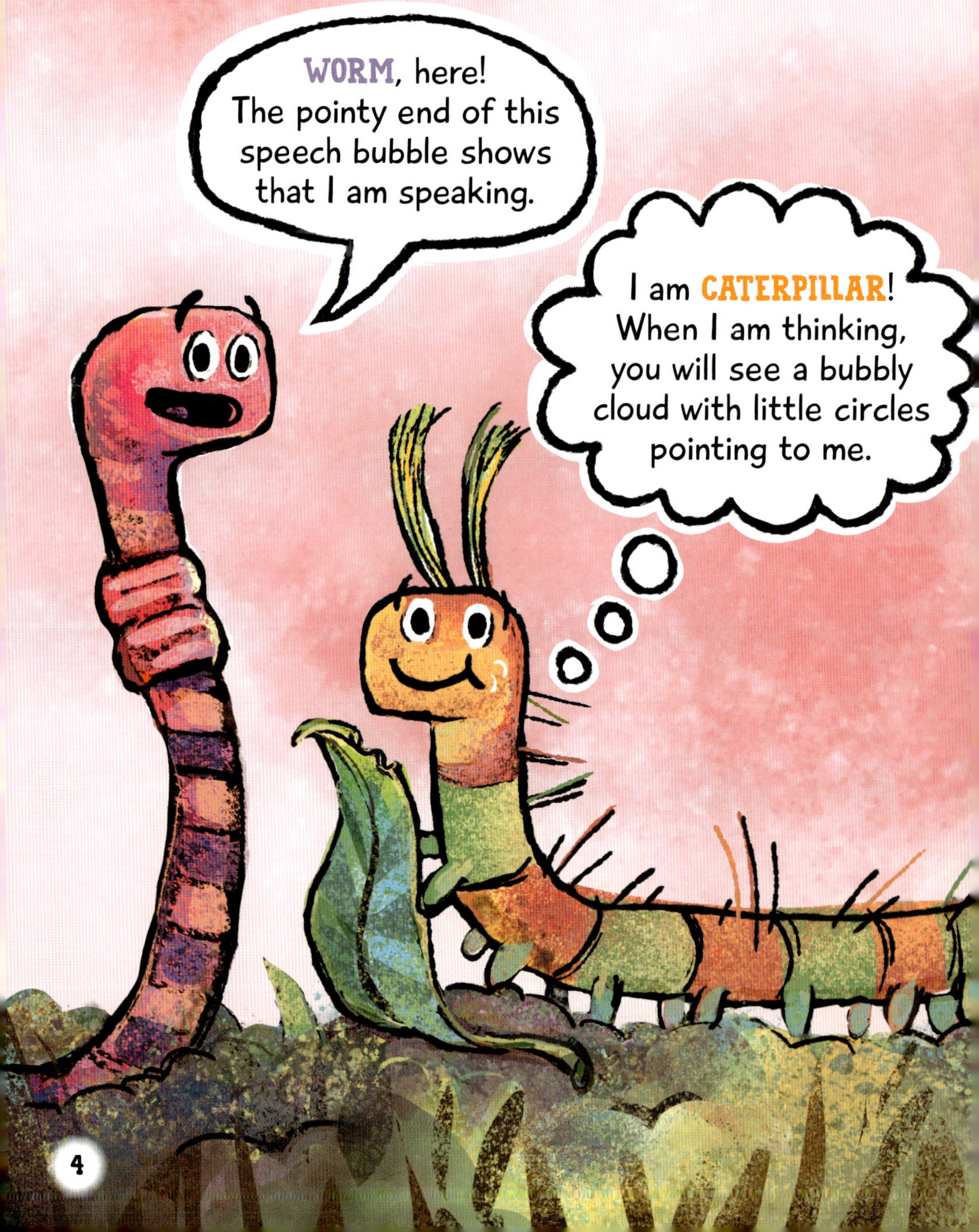
WORM, here! The pointy end of this speech bubble shows that I am speaking.
I am CATERPILLAR! When I am thinking, you will see a bubbly cloud with little circles pointing to me.

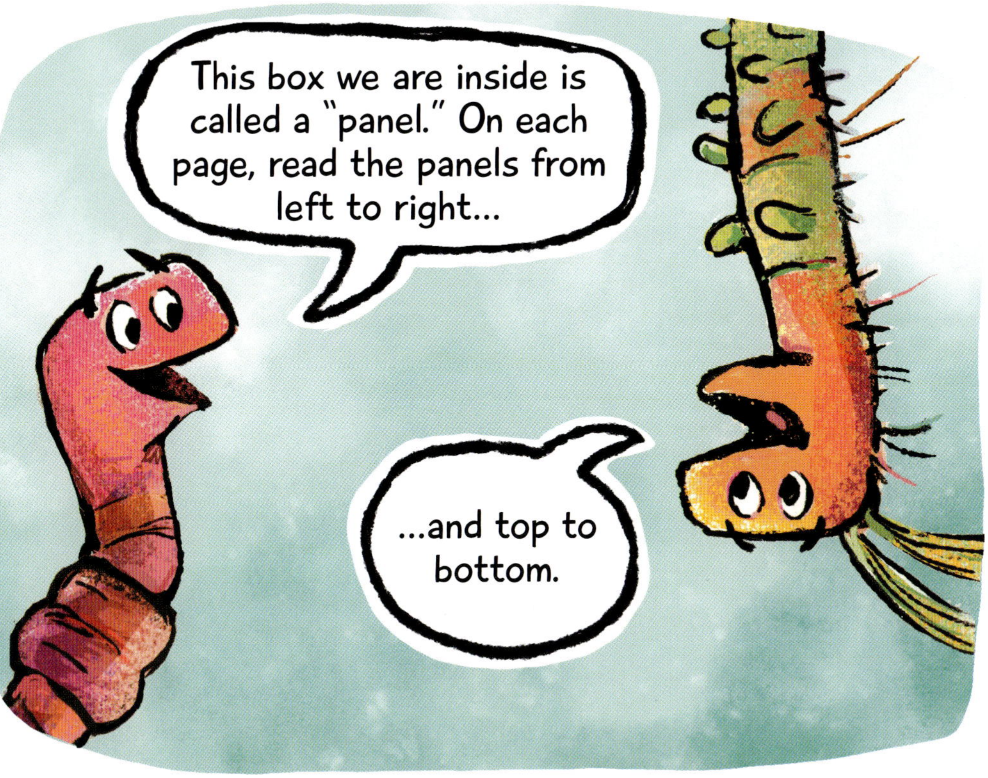
This box we are inside is called a "panel." On each page, read the panels from left to right...
...and top to bottom.

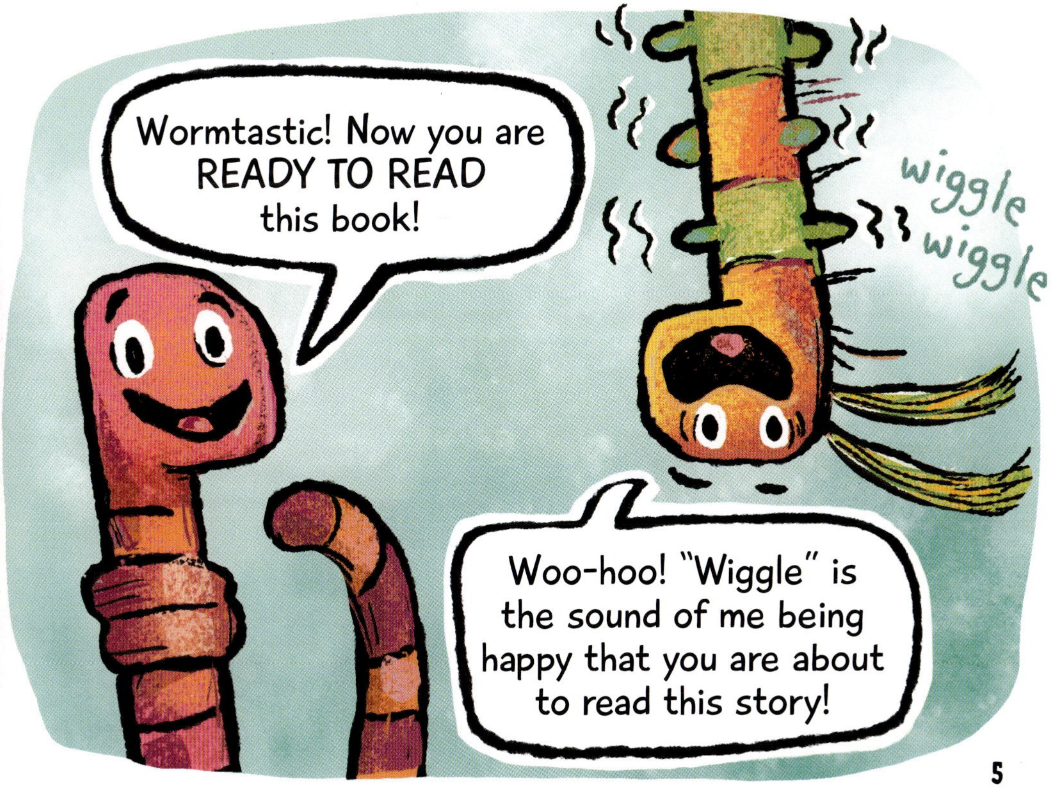
Wormtastic! Now you are READY TO READ this book!
wiggle wiggle
Woo-hoo! "Wiggle" is the sound of me being happy that you are about to read this story!

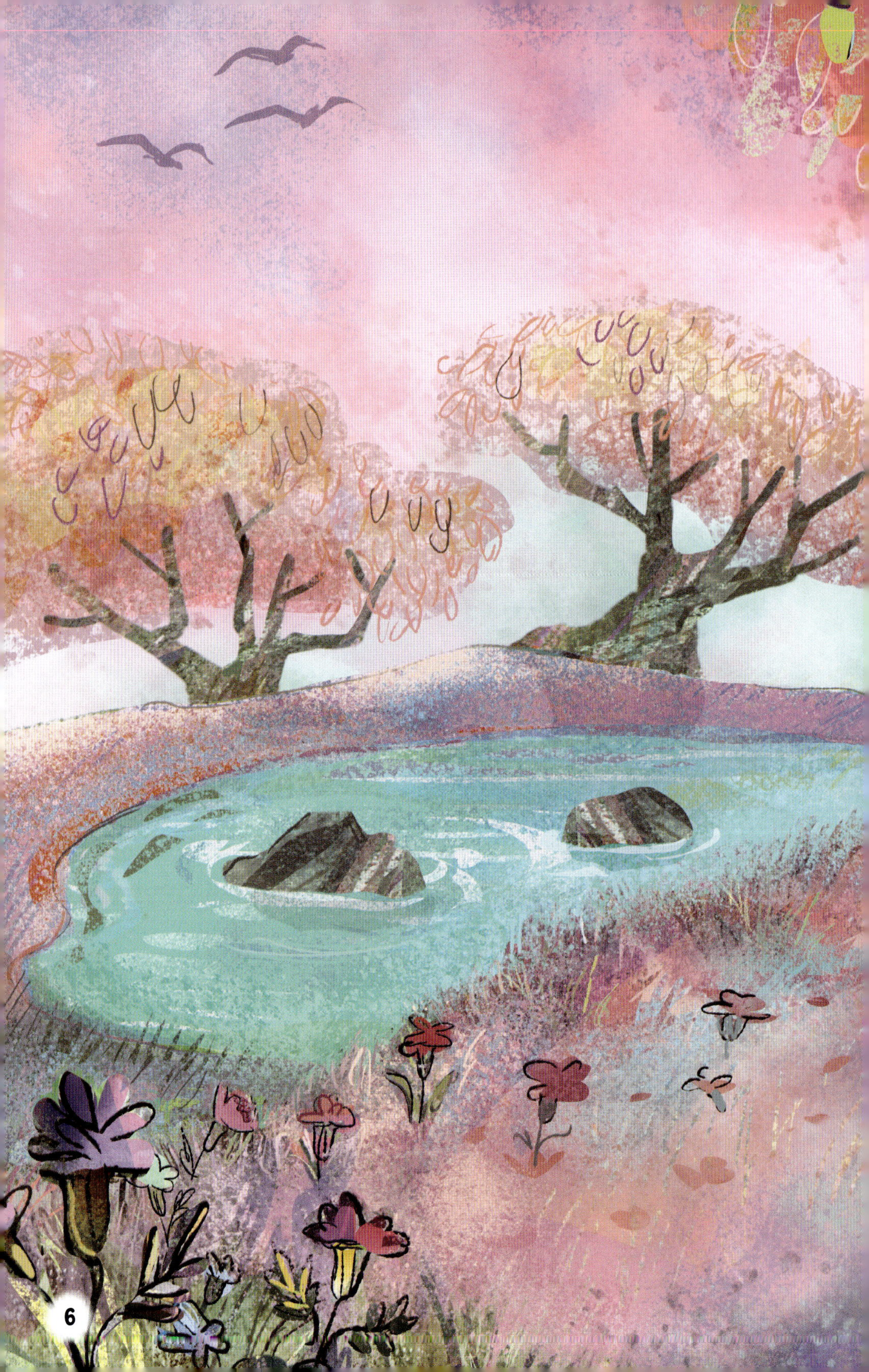

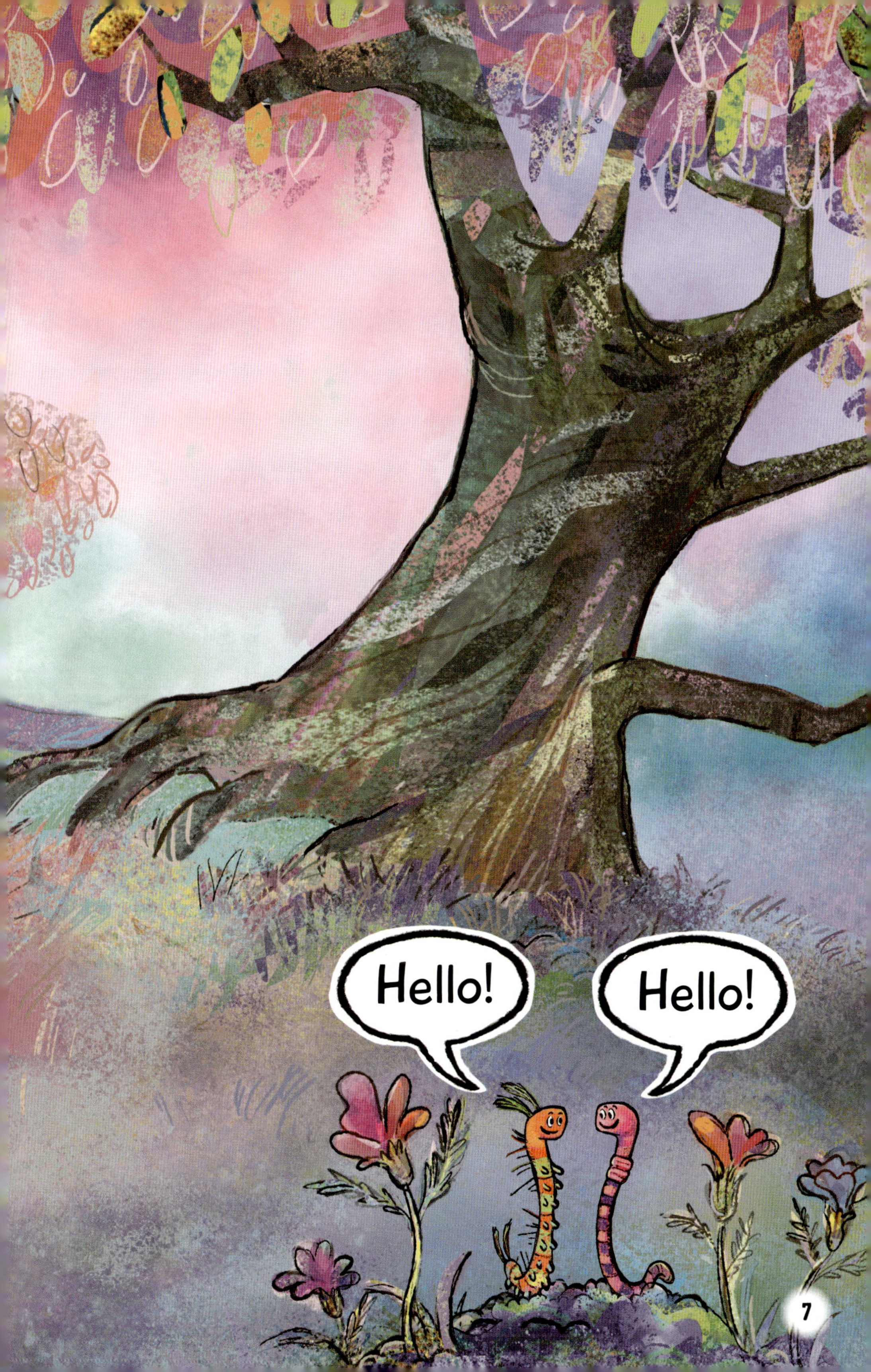
Hello!
Hello!

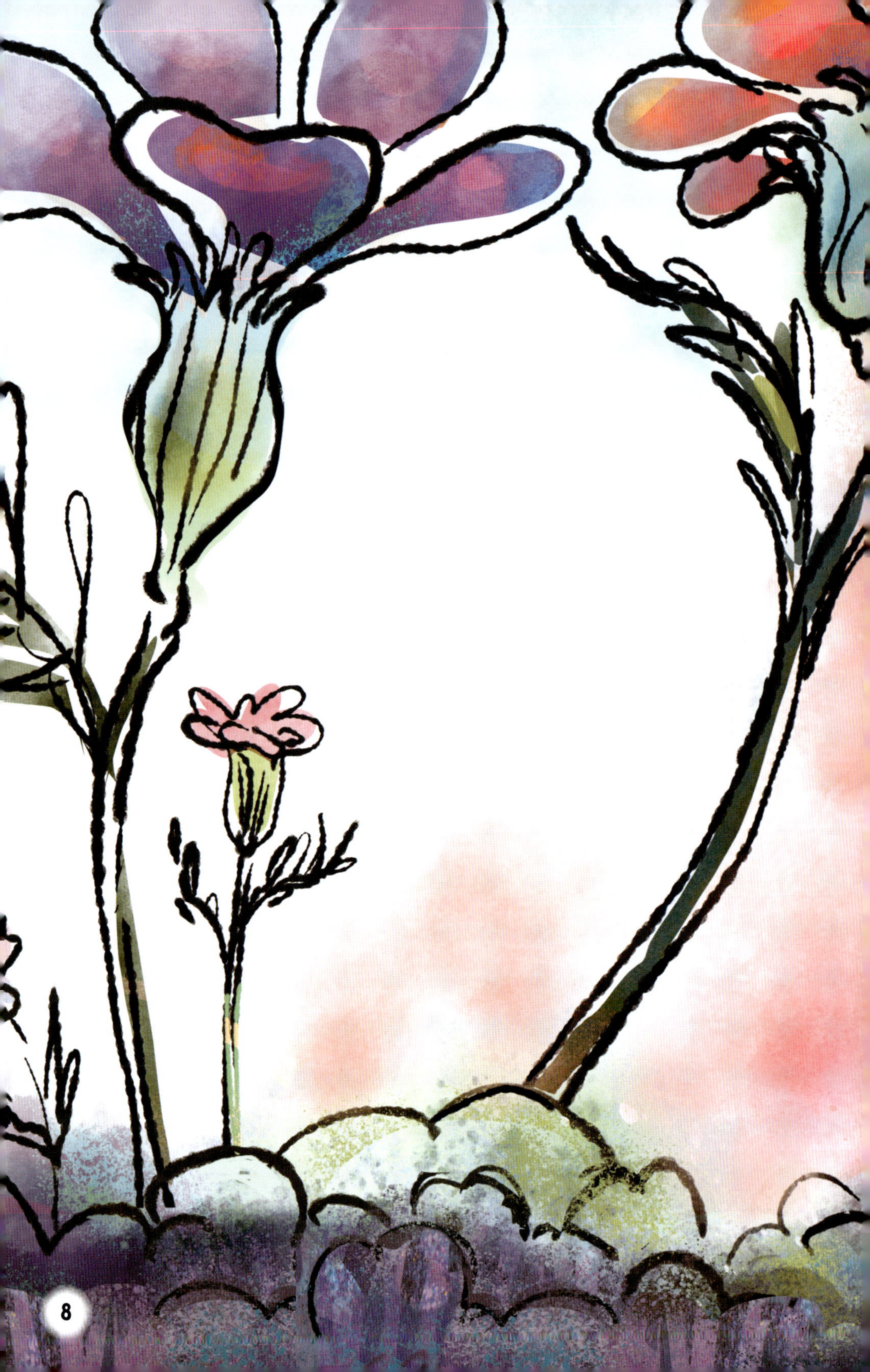

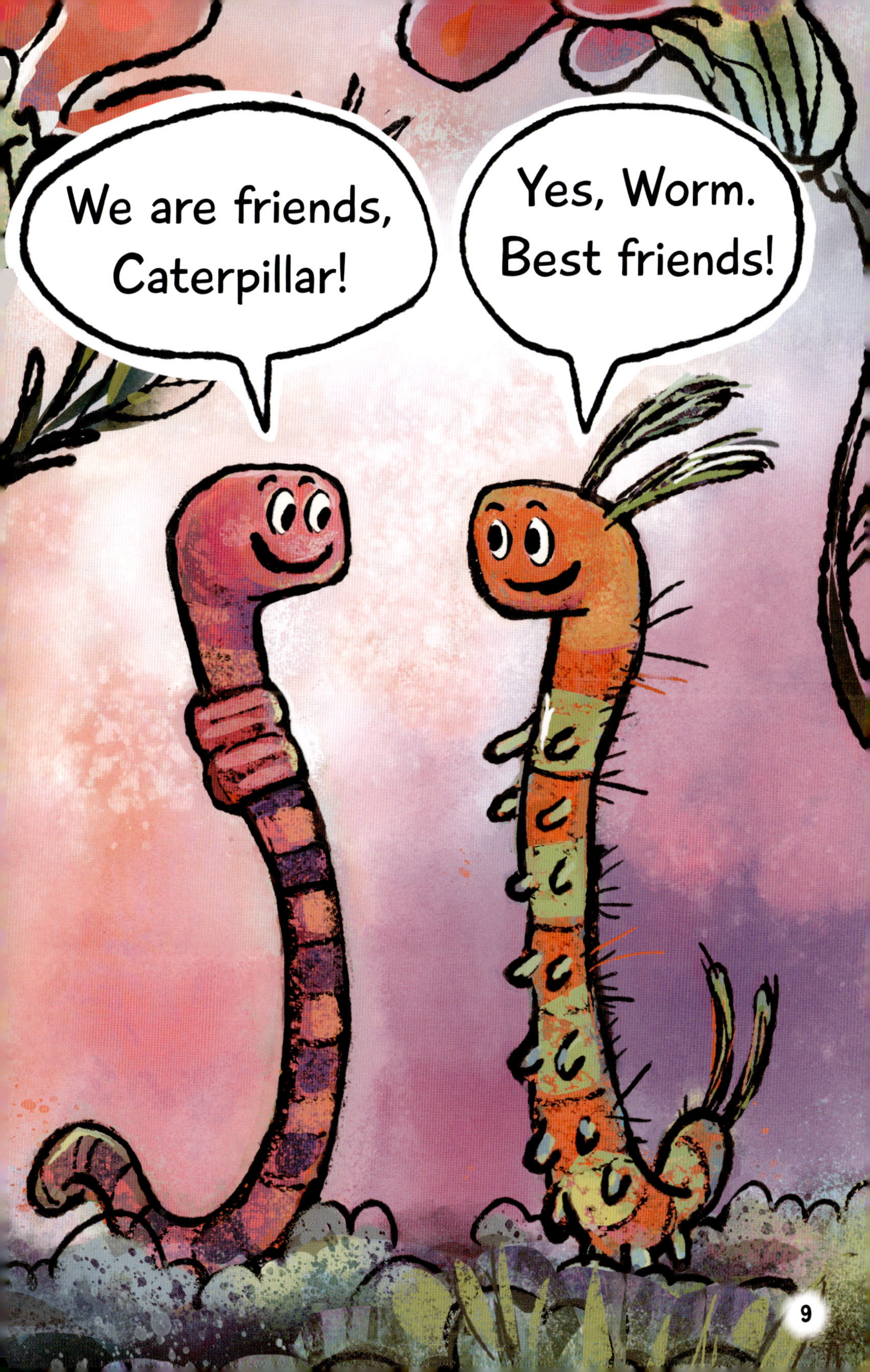
We are friends, Caterpillar!
Yes, Worm. Best friends!

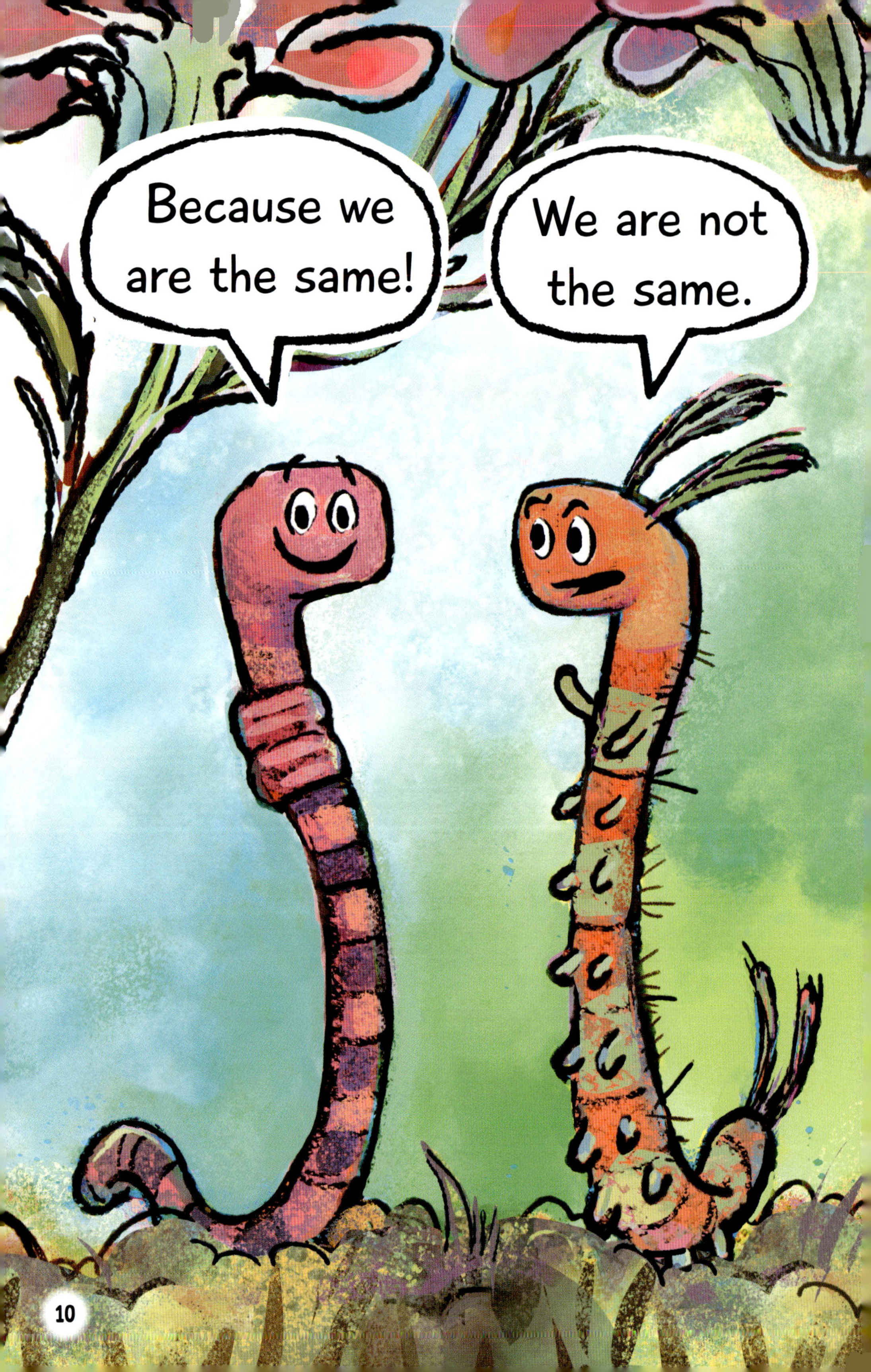
Because we are the same!
We are not the same.

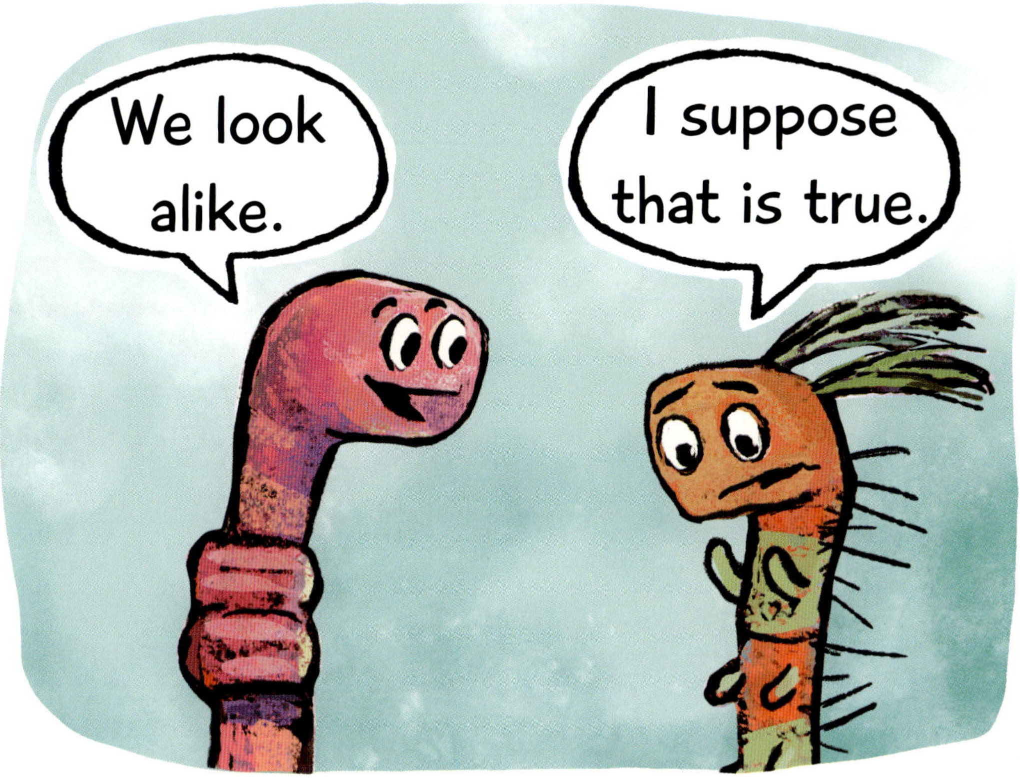
We look alike.
I suppose that is true.

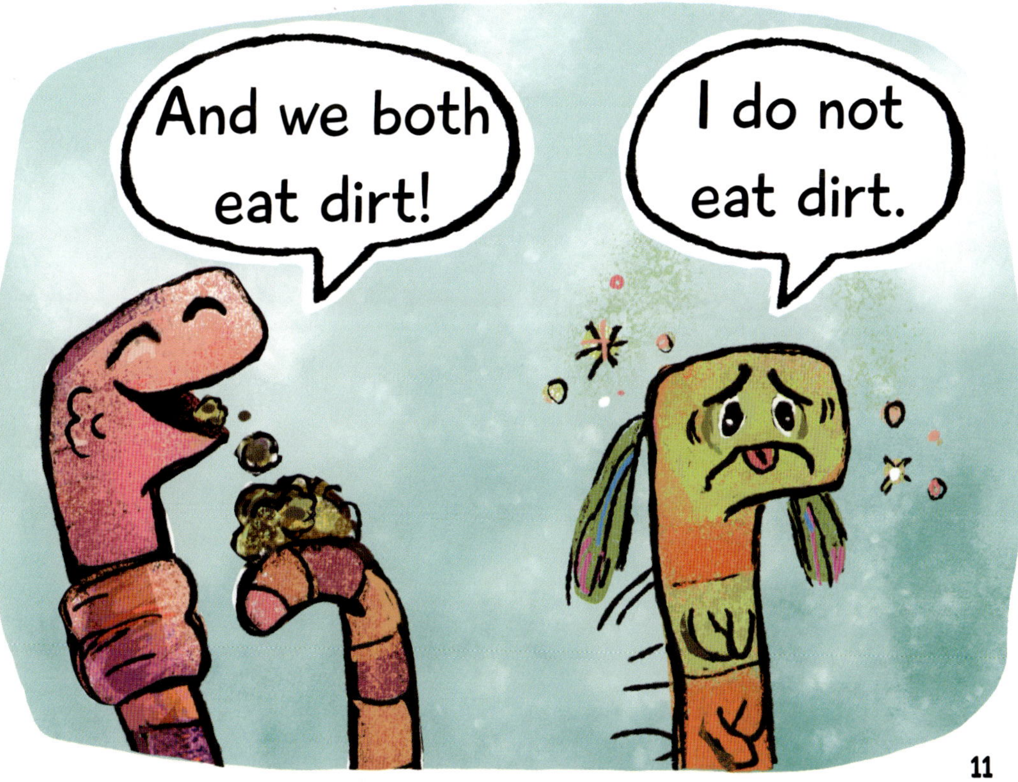
And we both eat dirt!
I do not eat dirt.

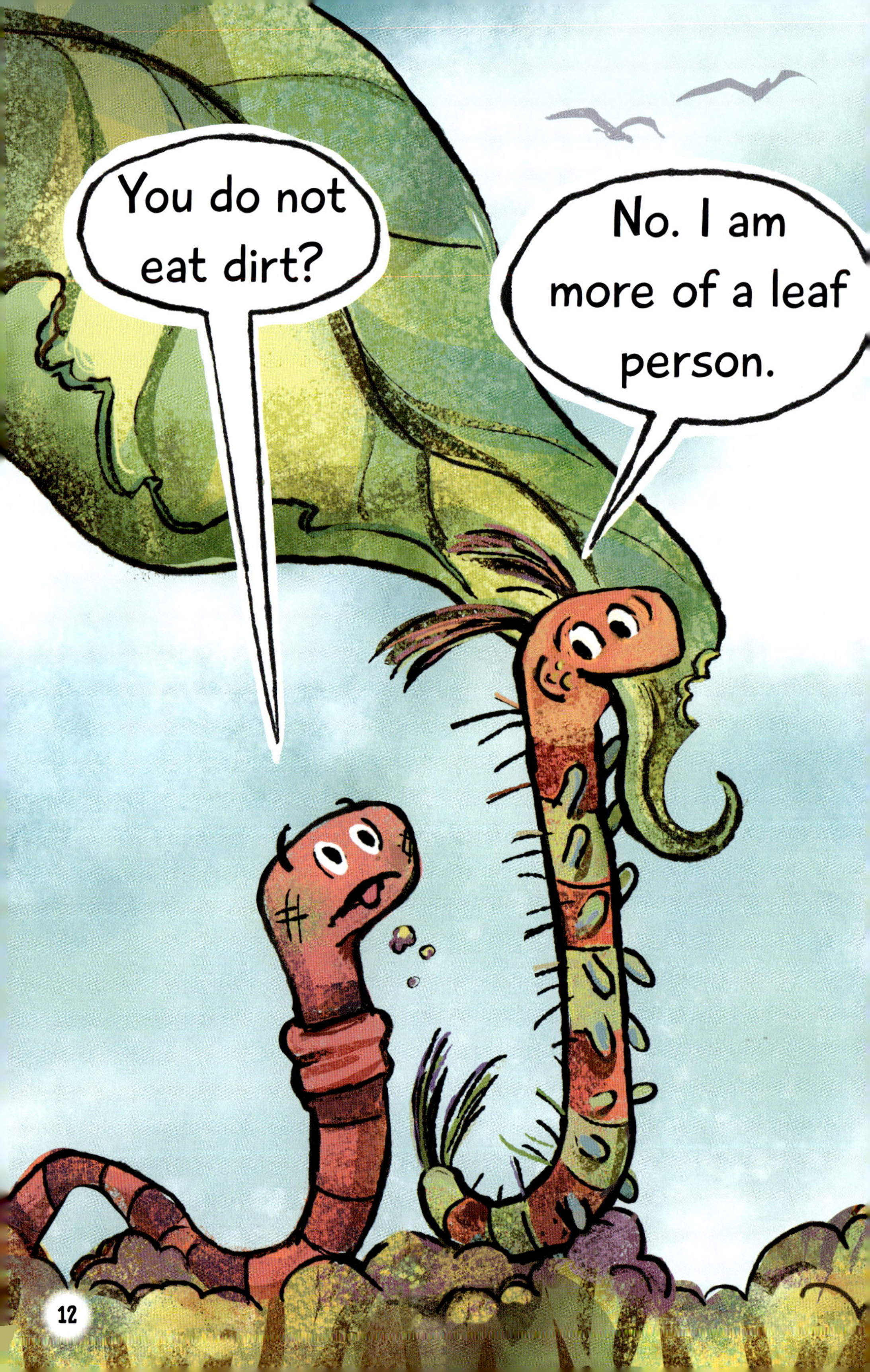
You do not eat dirt?
No. I am more of a leaf person.

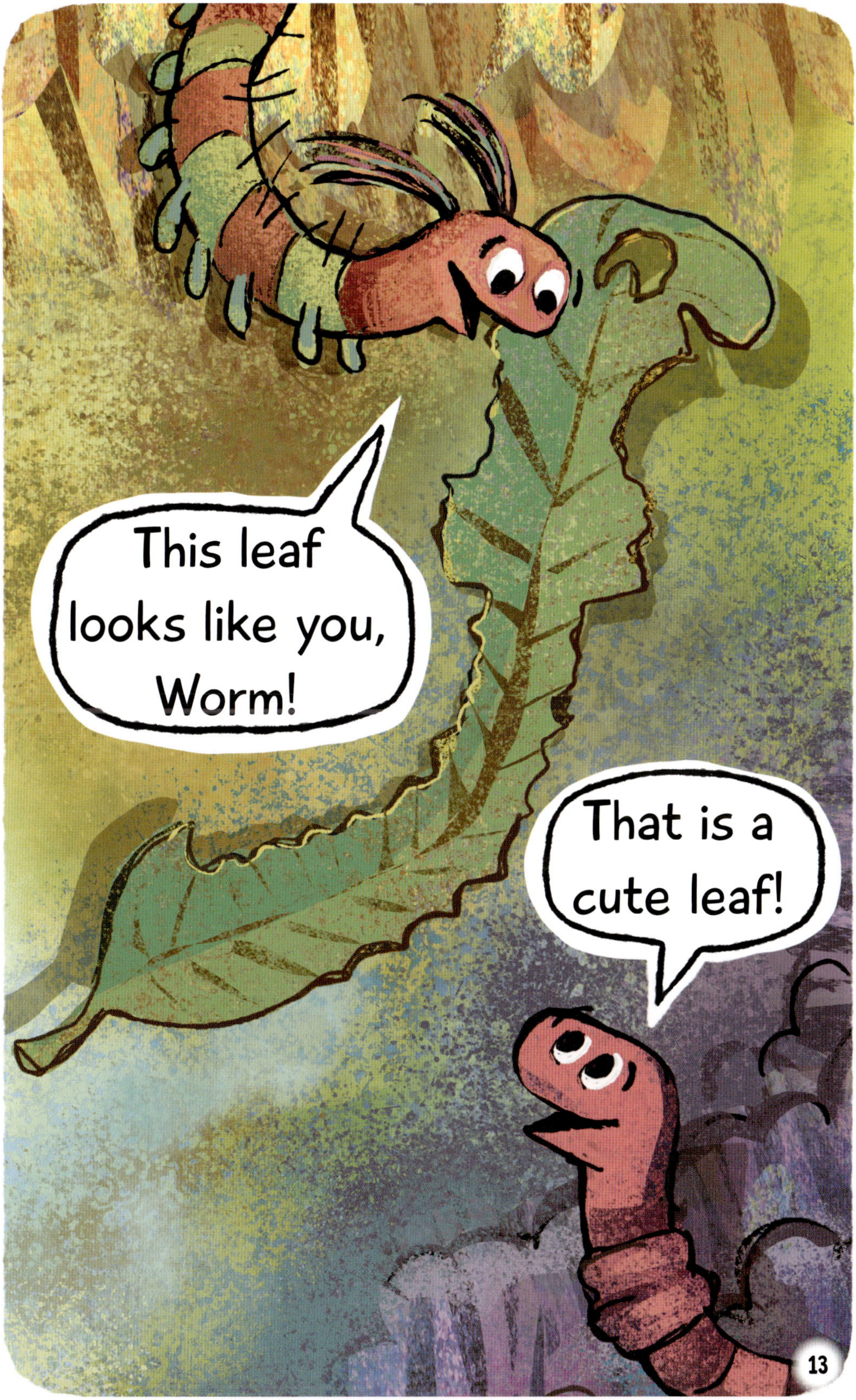
This leaf looks like you, Worm!
That is a cute leaf!

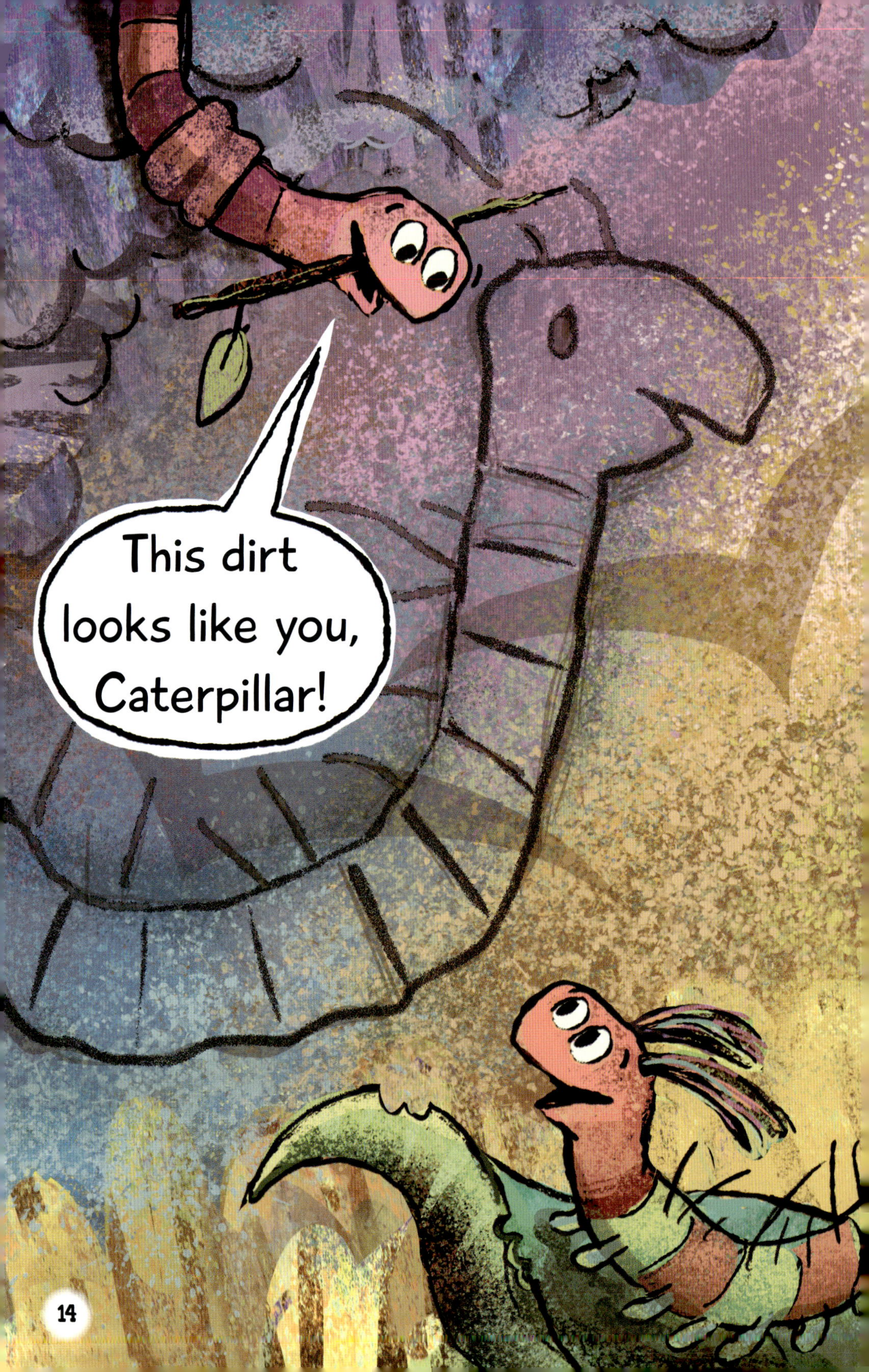
This dirt looks like you, Caterpillar!

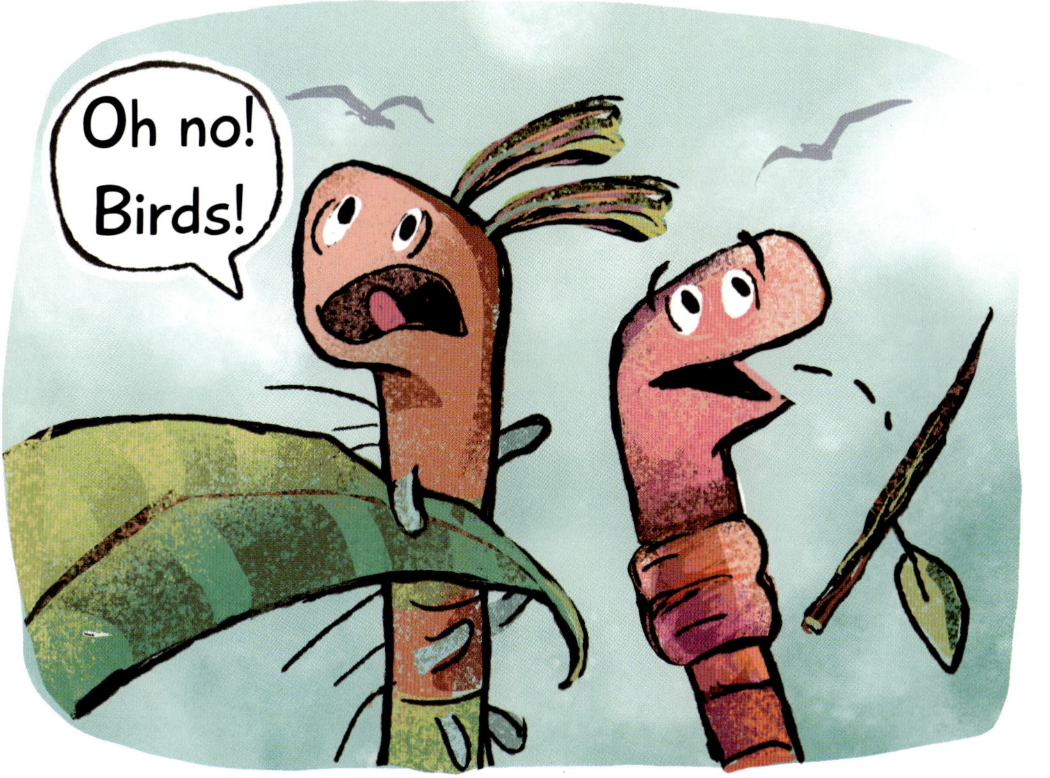
Oh no!
Birds!

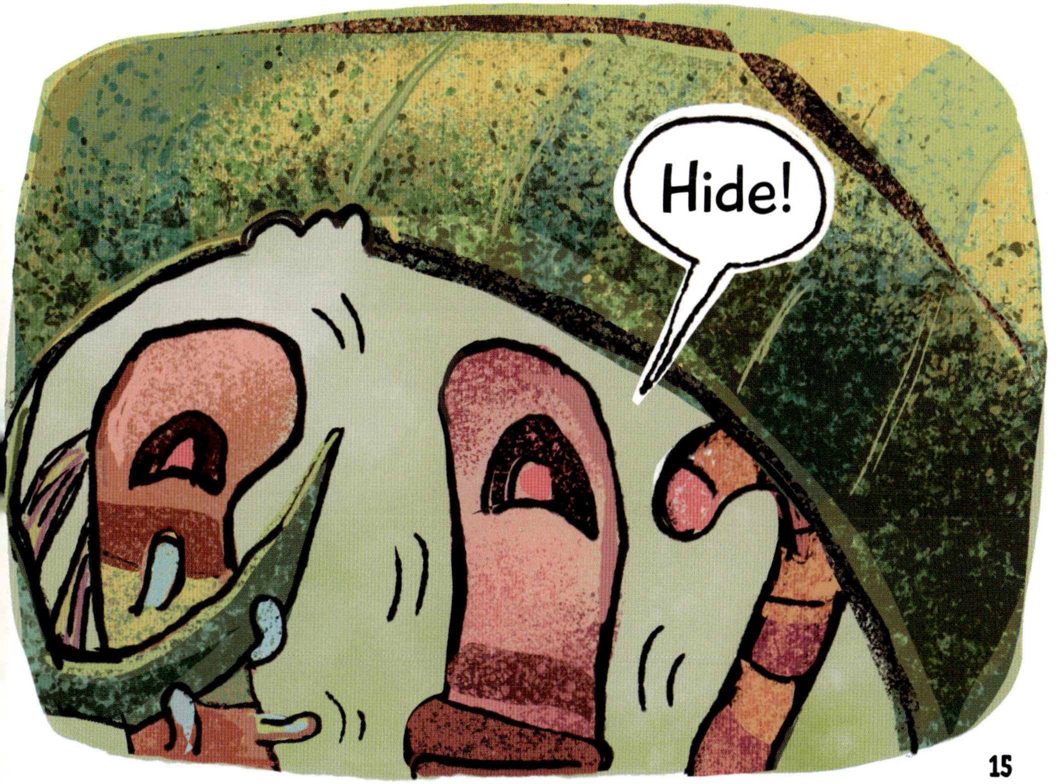
Hide!

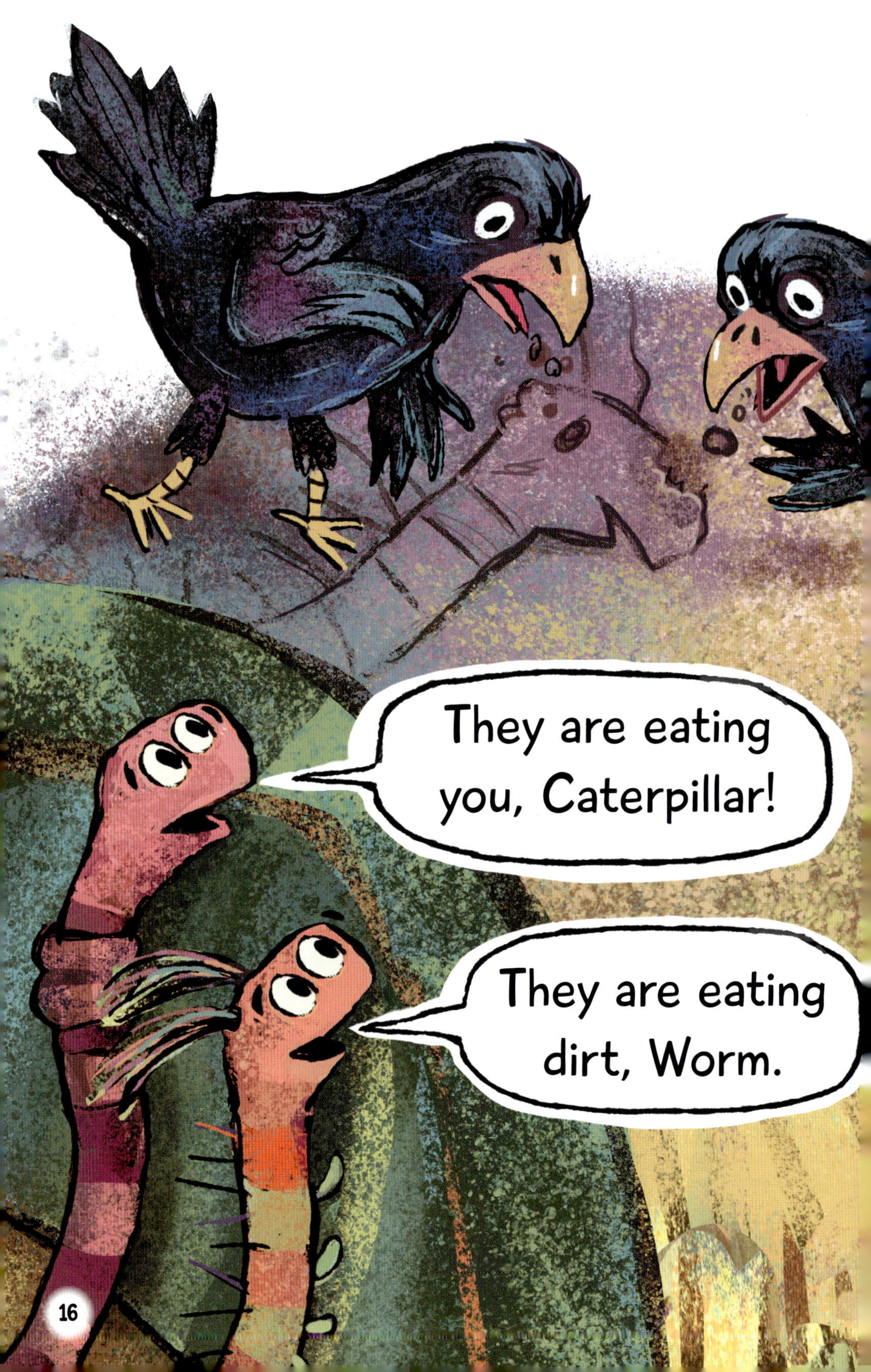
They are eating you, Caterpillar!
They are eating dirt, Worm.

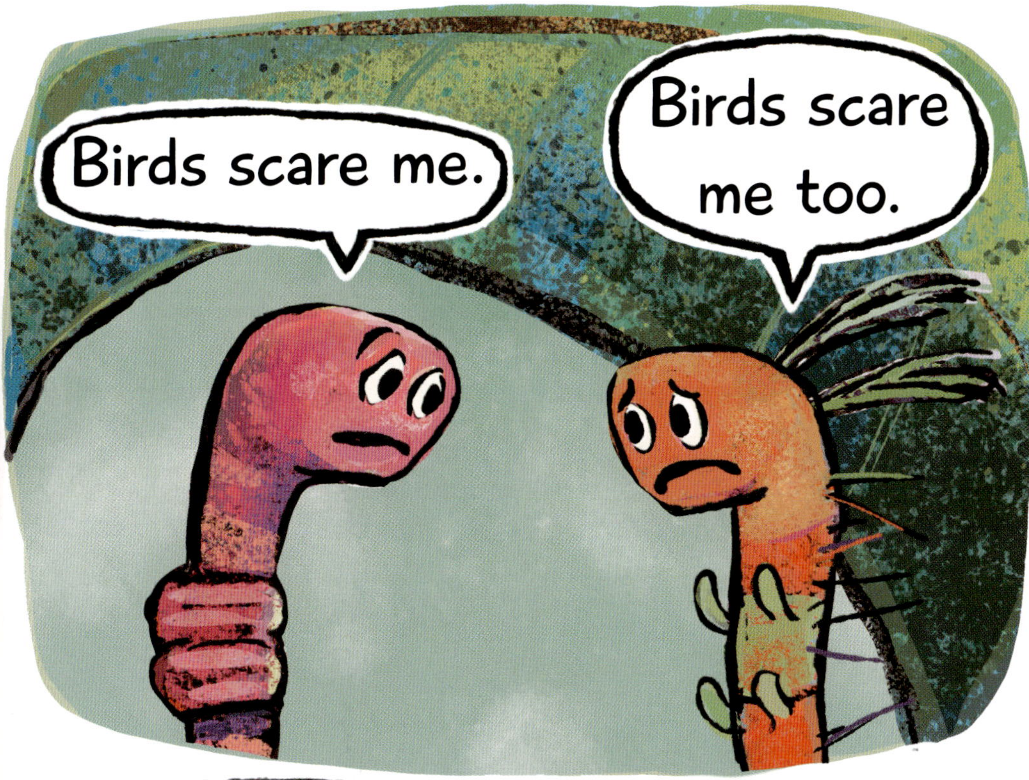
Birds scare me.
Birds scare me too.

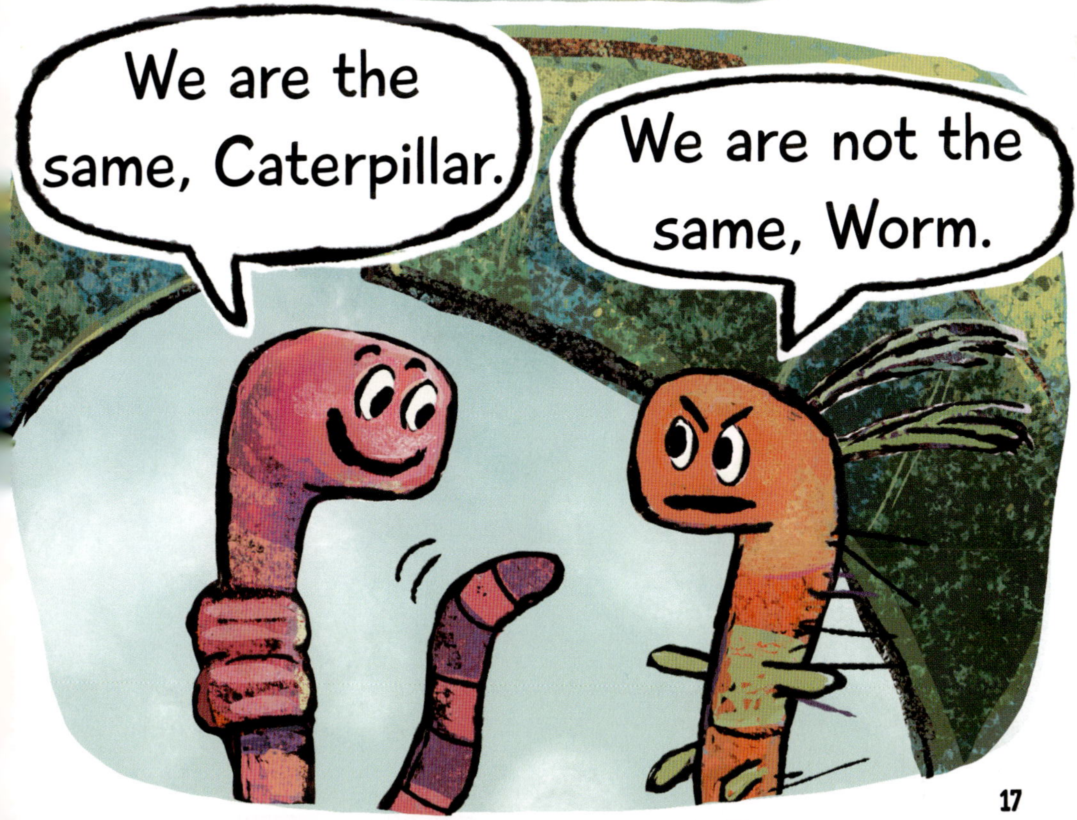
We are the same, Caterpillar.
We are not the same, Worm.

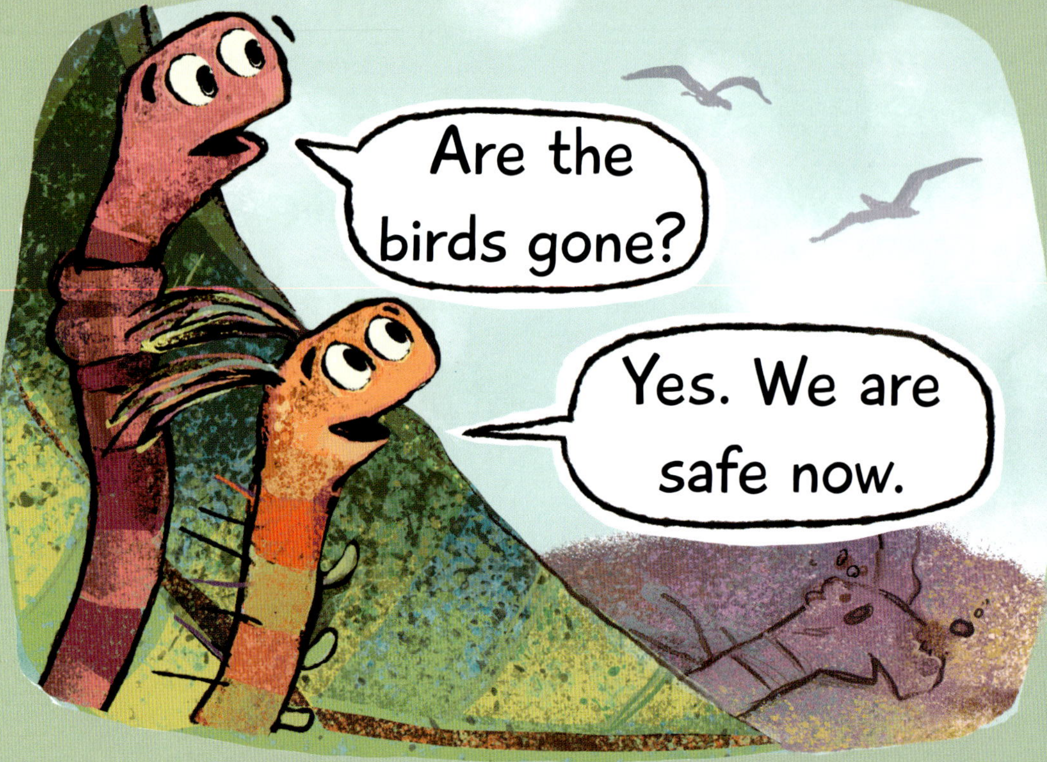
Are the birds gone?
Yes. We are safe now.

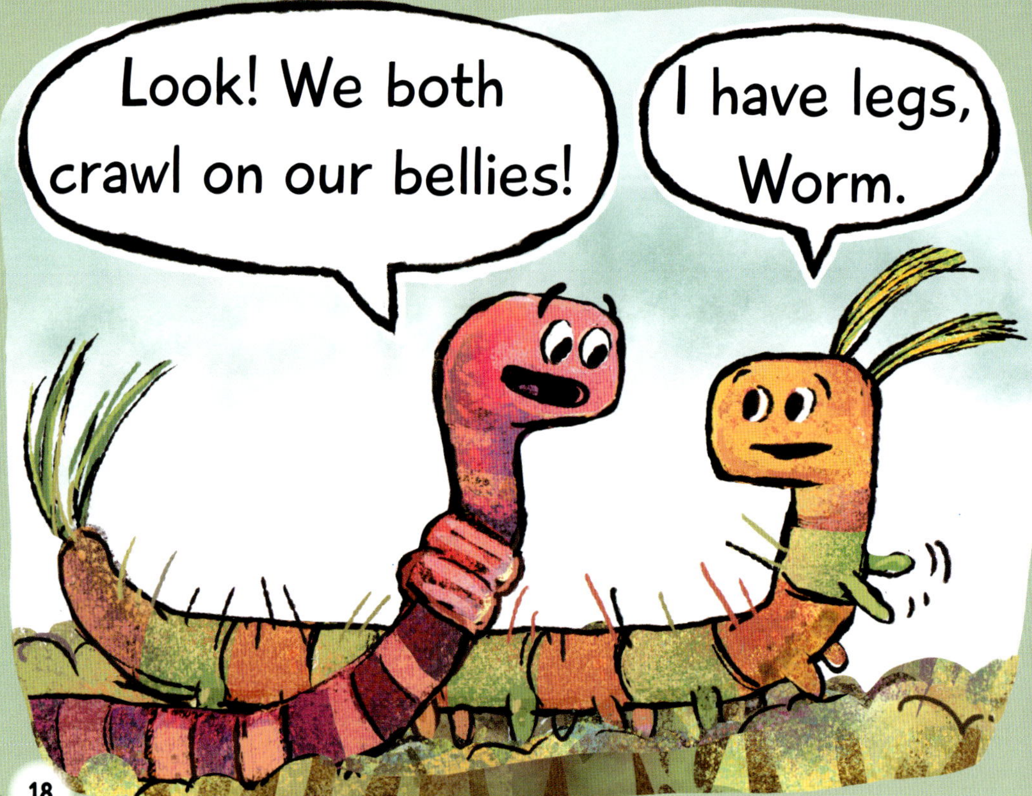
Look! We both crawl on our bellies!
I have legs, Worm.

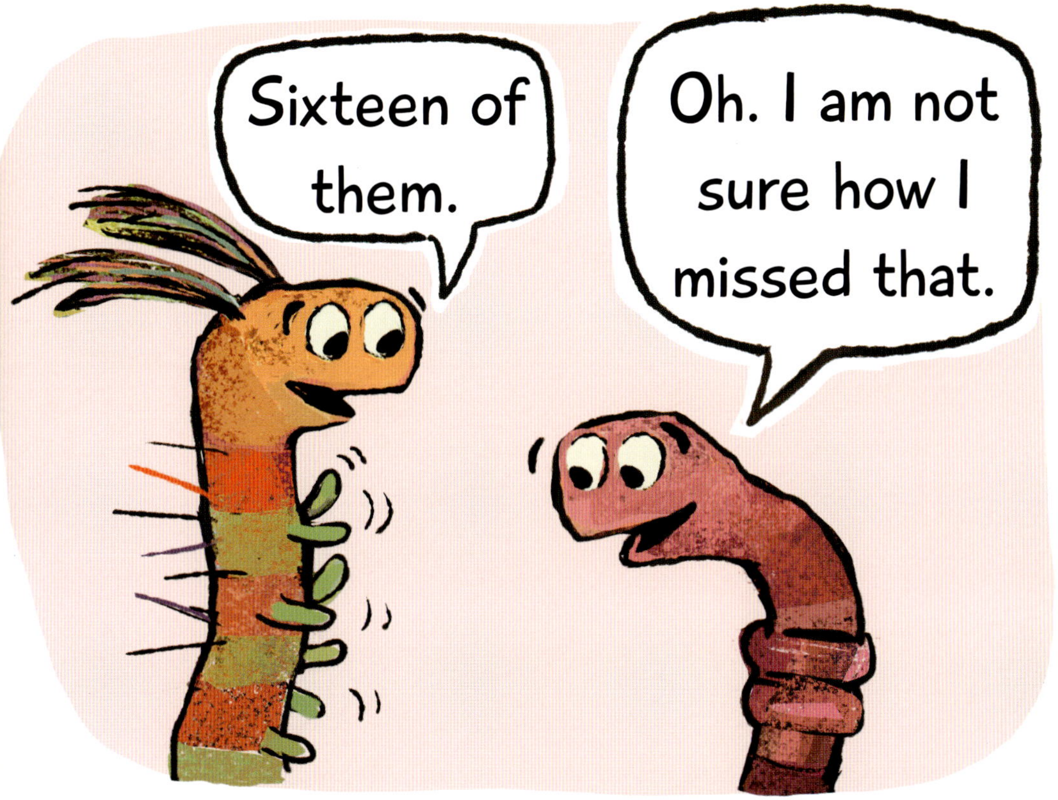
Sixteen of them.
Oh. I am not sure how I missed that.

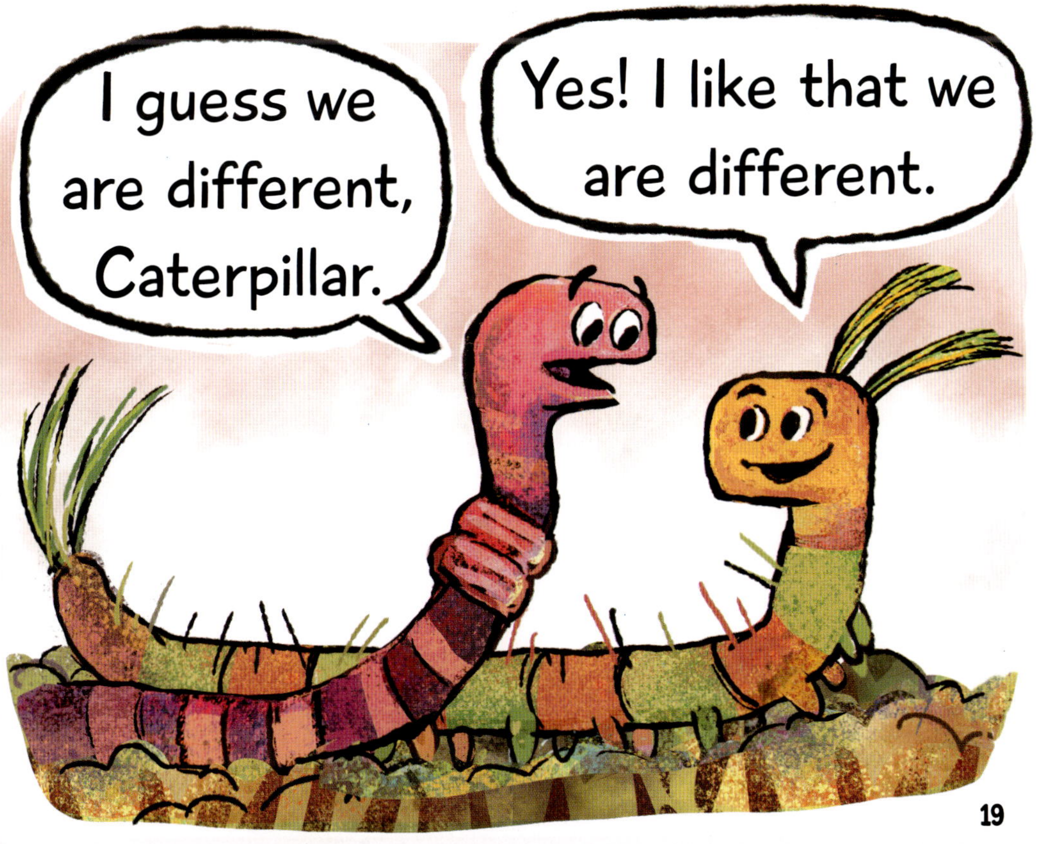
I guess we are different, Caterpillar.
Yes! I like that we are different.

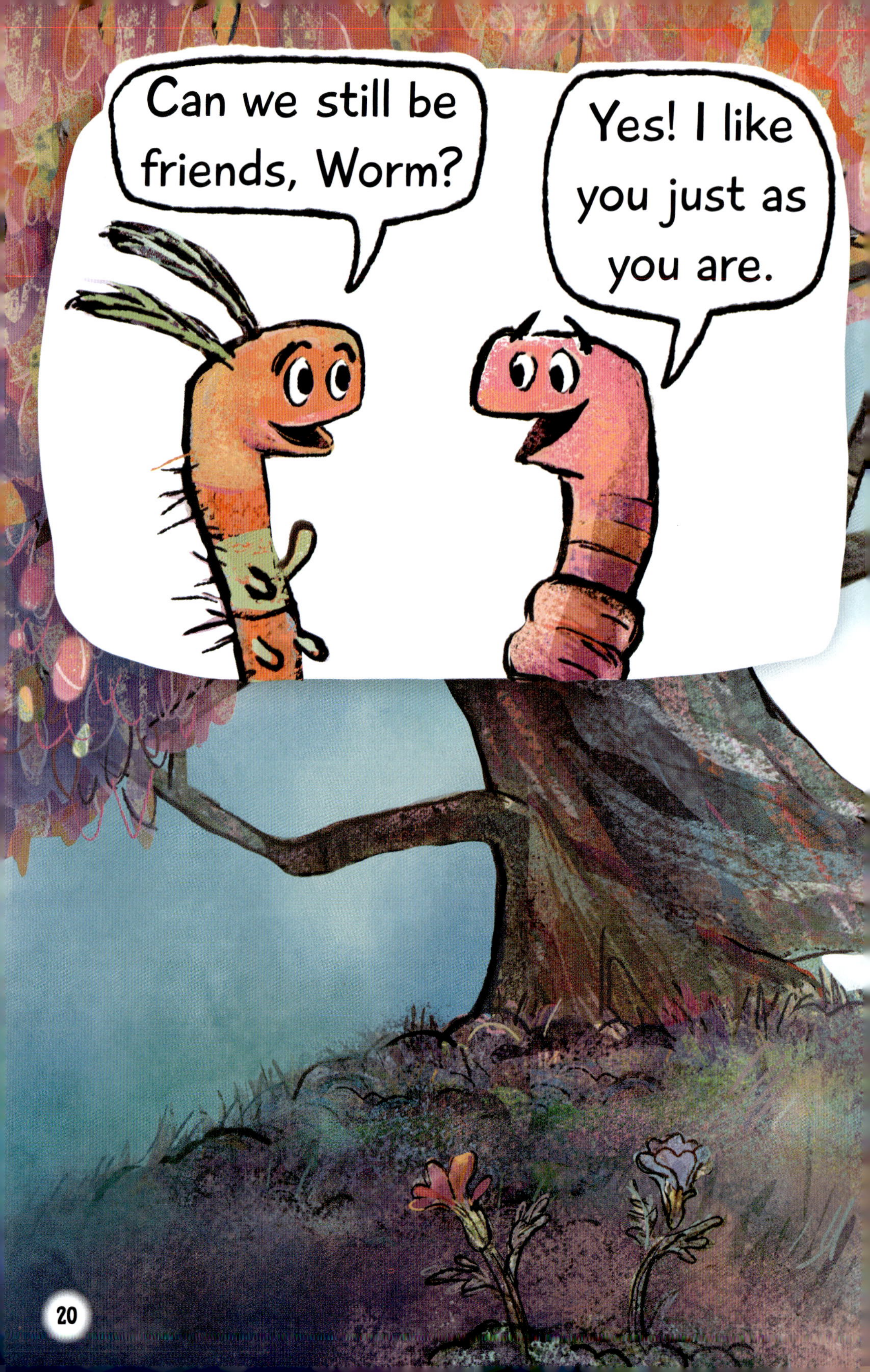
Can we still be friends, Worm?
Yes! I like you just as you are.

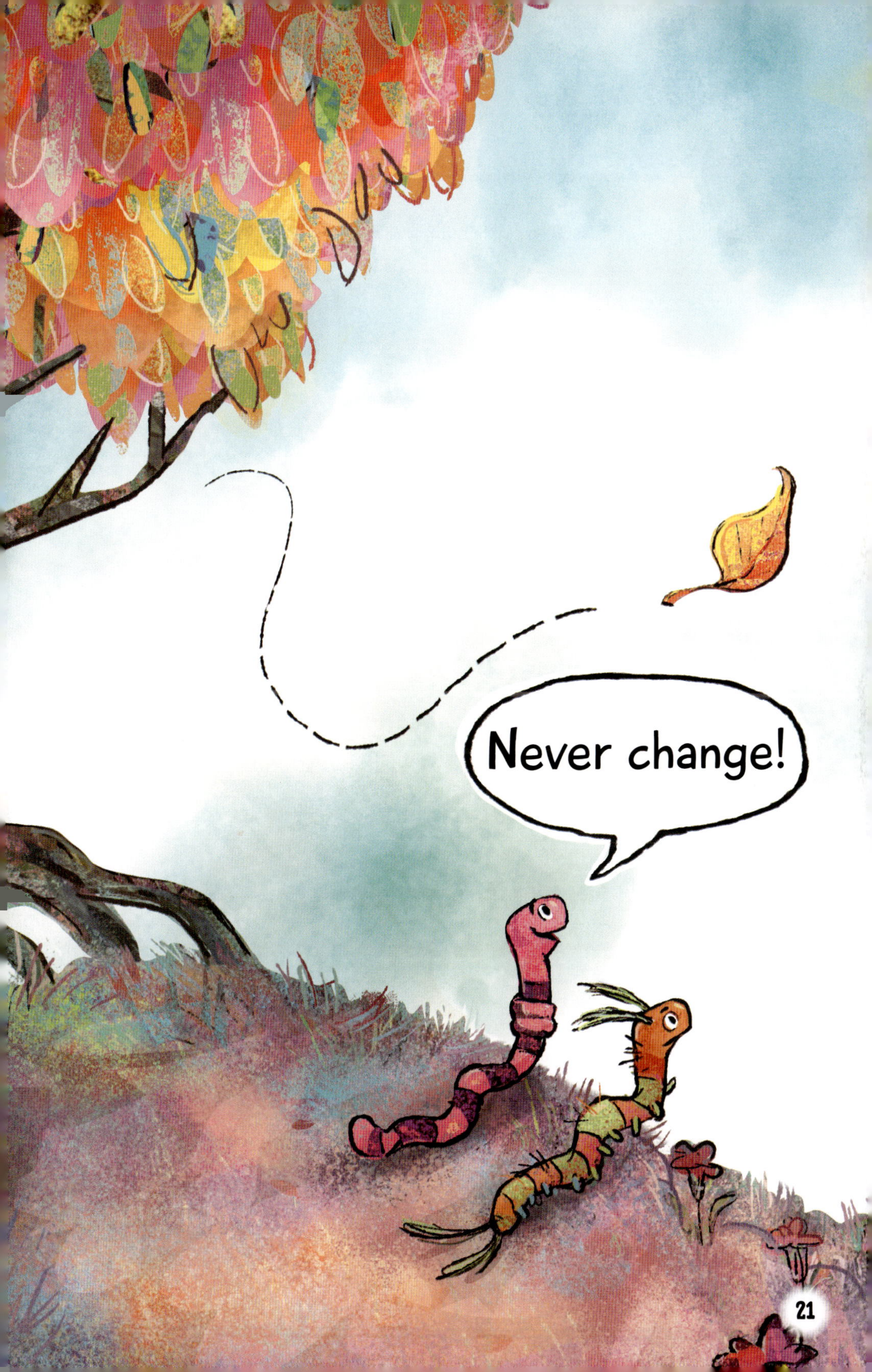
Never change!

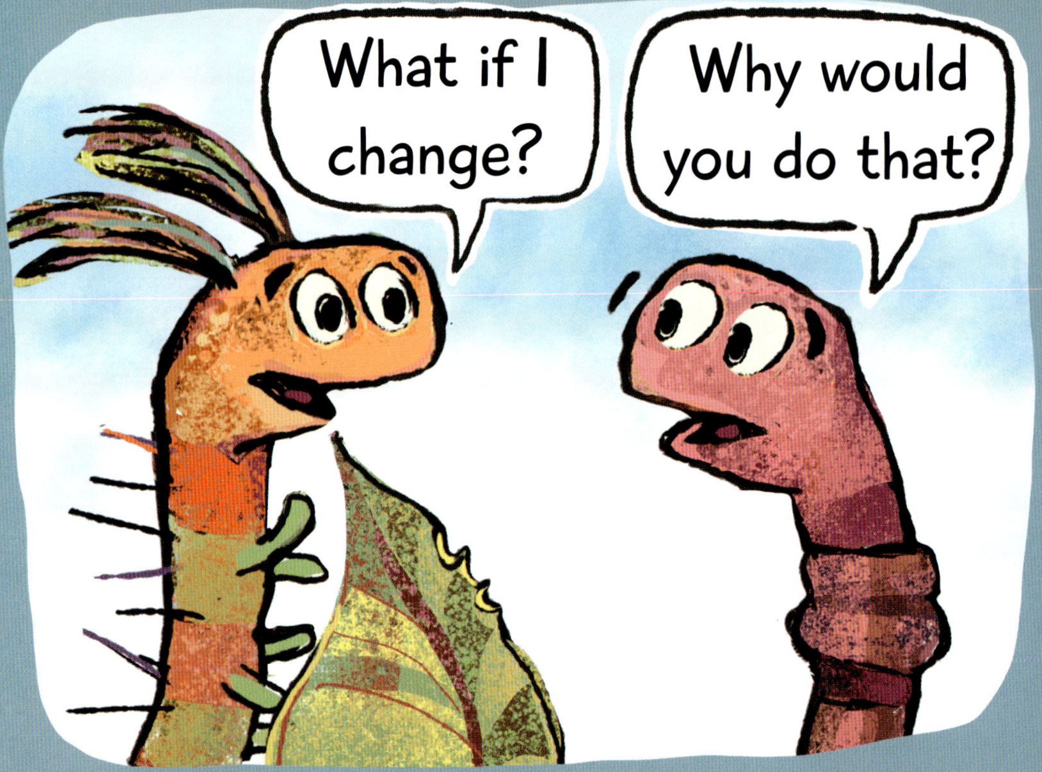
What if I change?
Why would you do that?

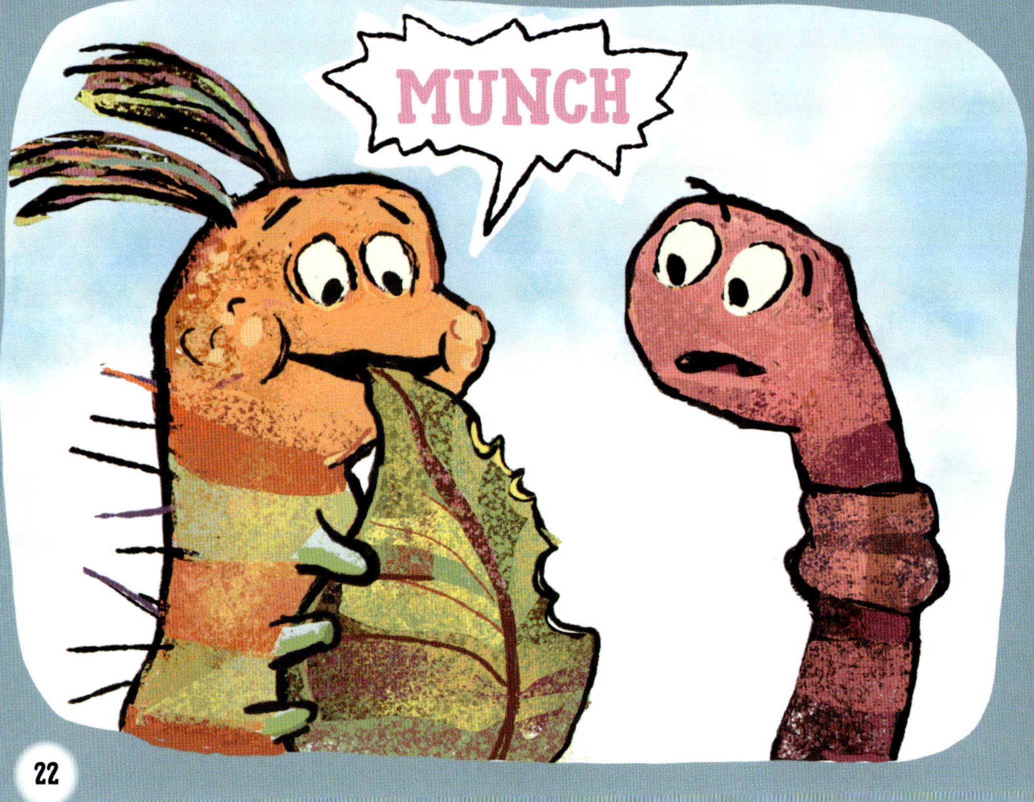
MUNCH

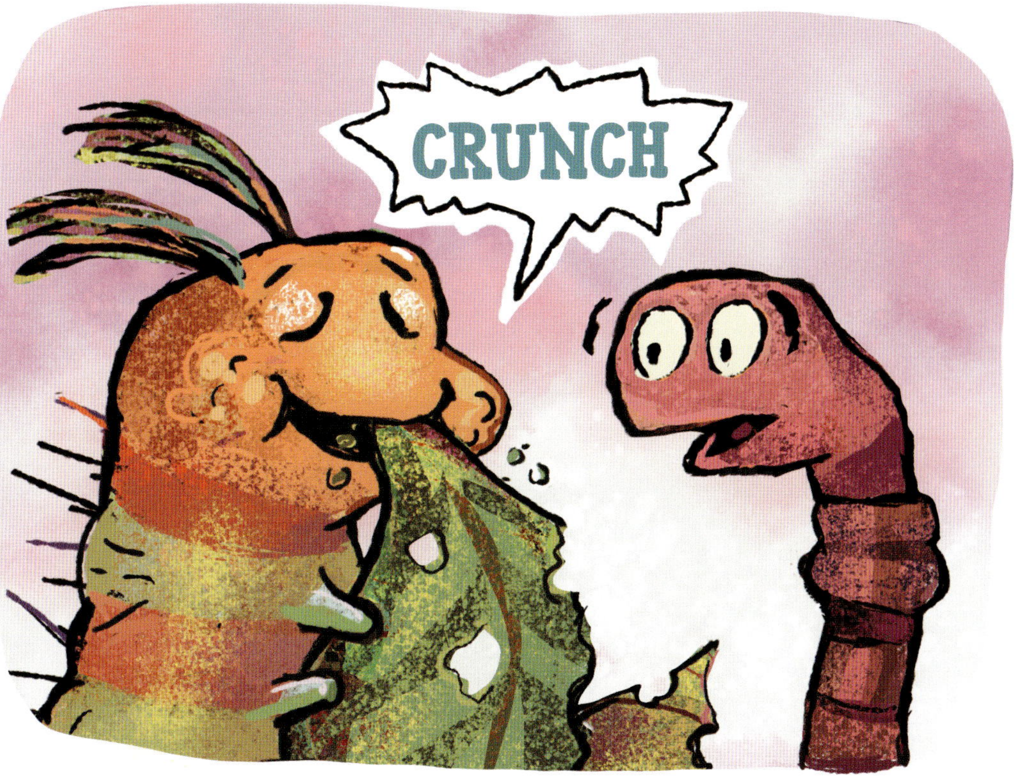
CRUNCH

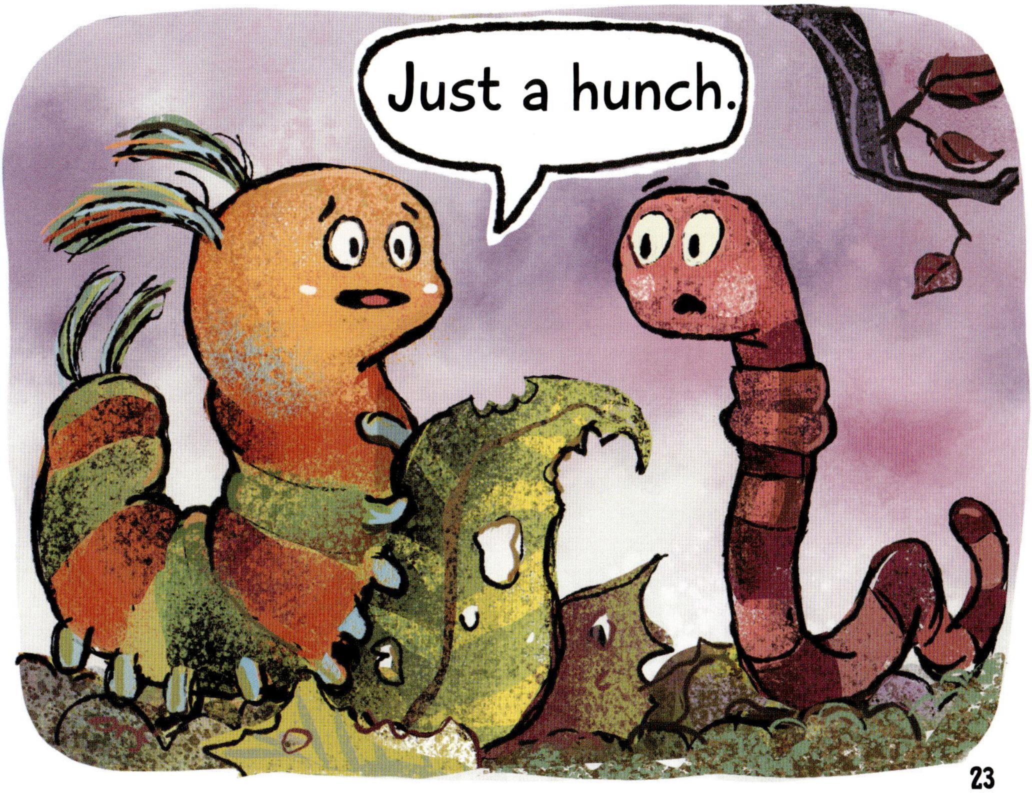
Just a hunch.

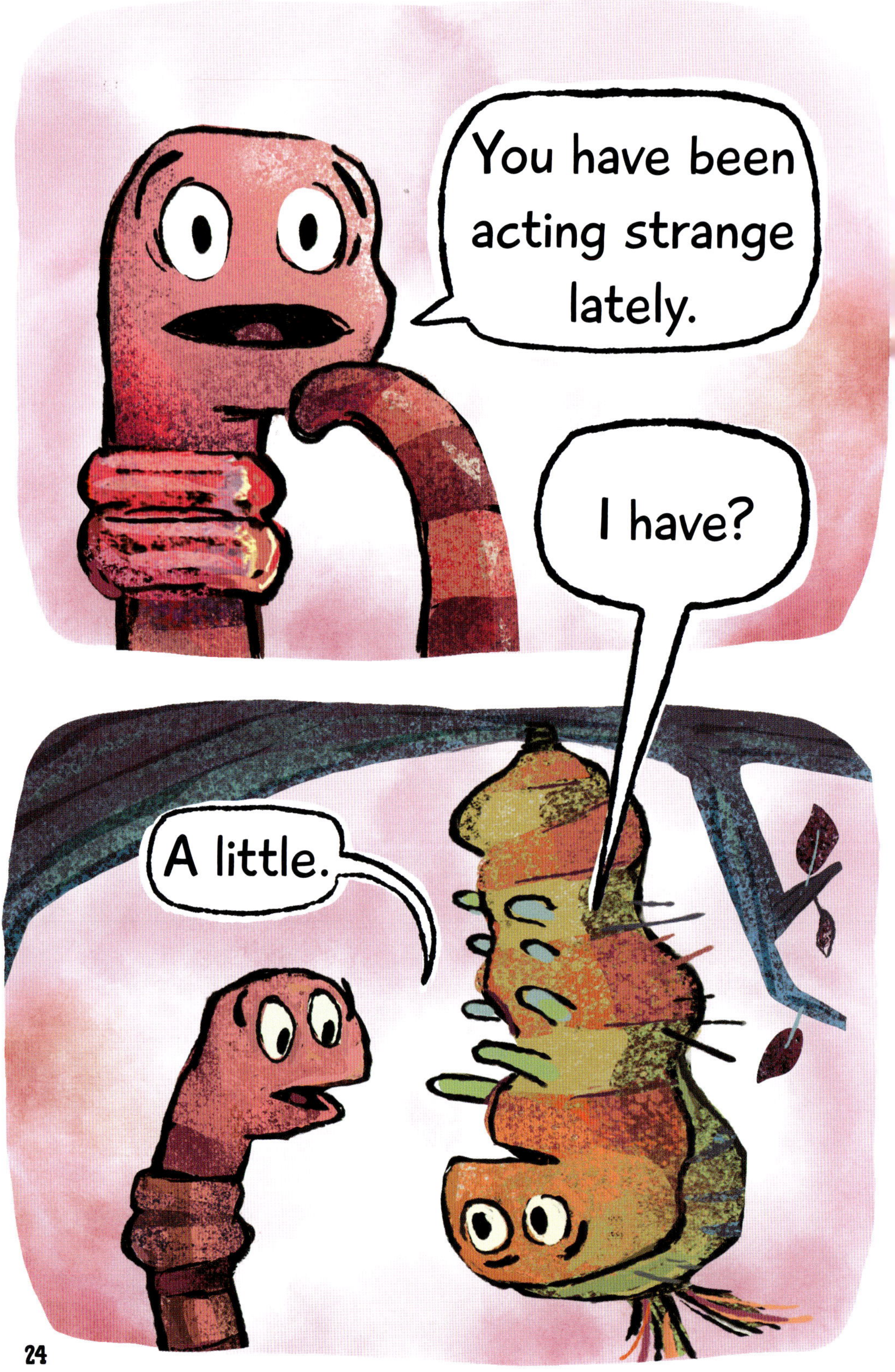
You have been acting strange lately.
I have?
A little.

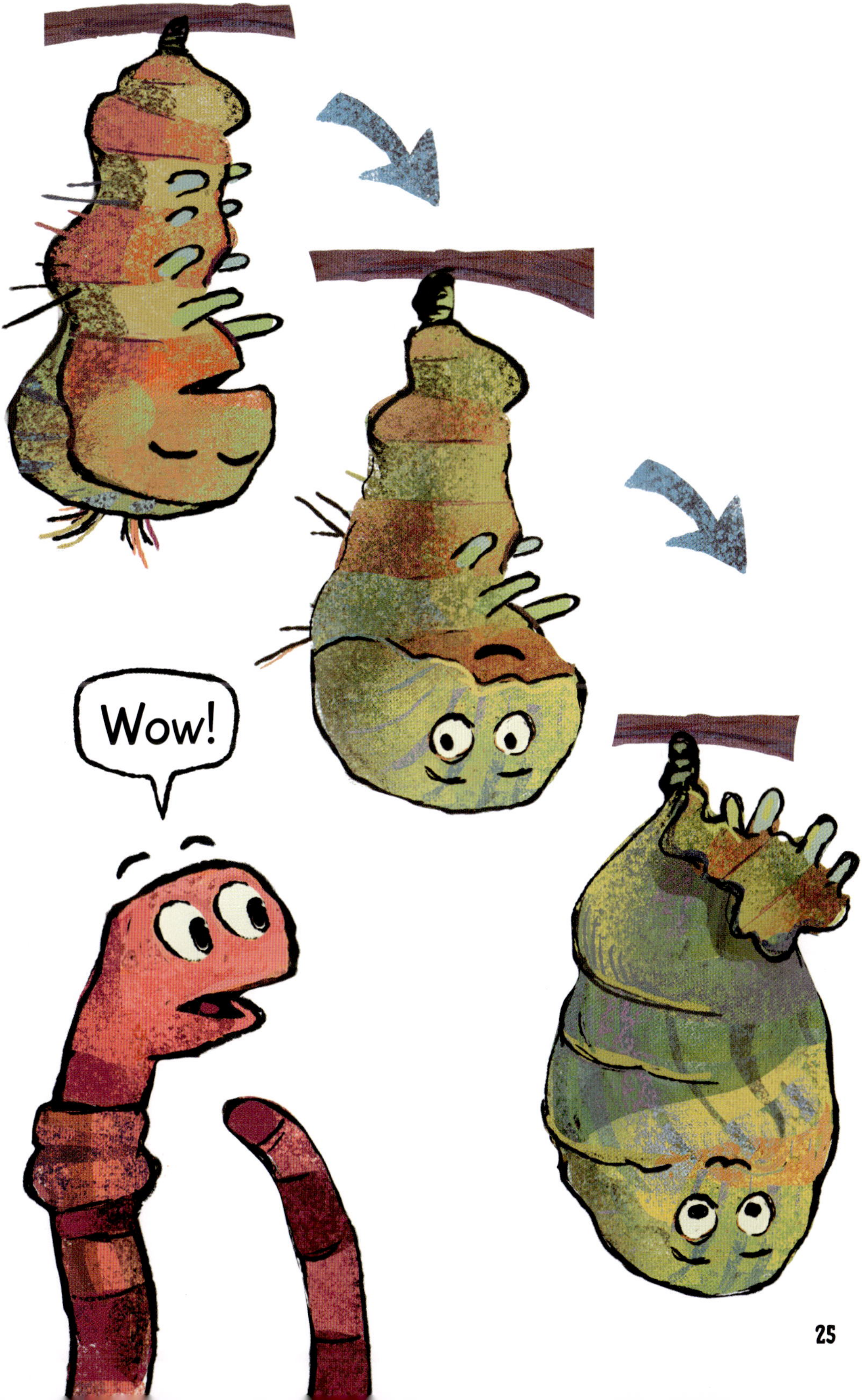
Wow!

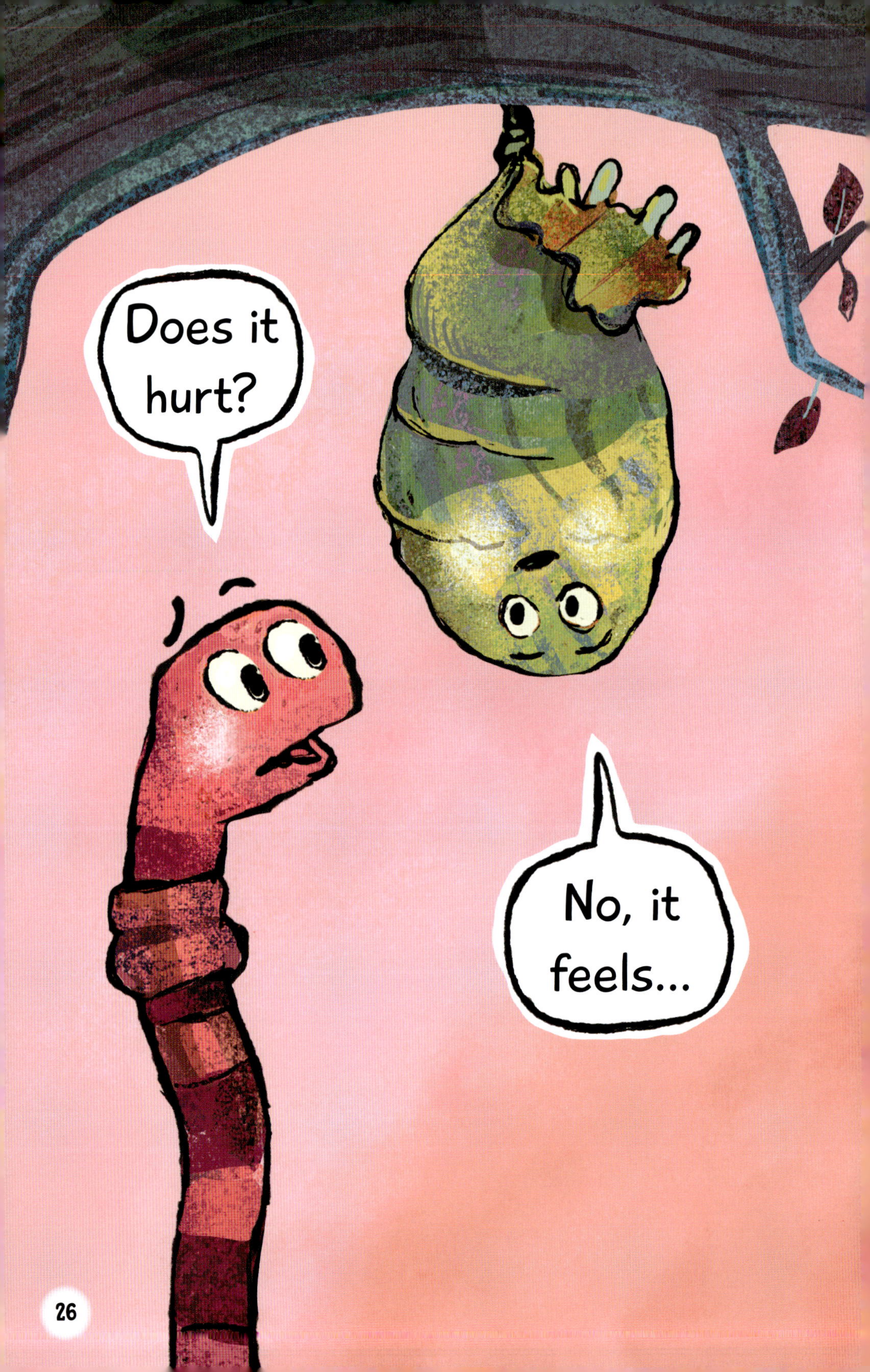
Does it hurt?
No, it feels...

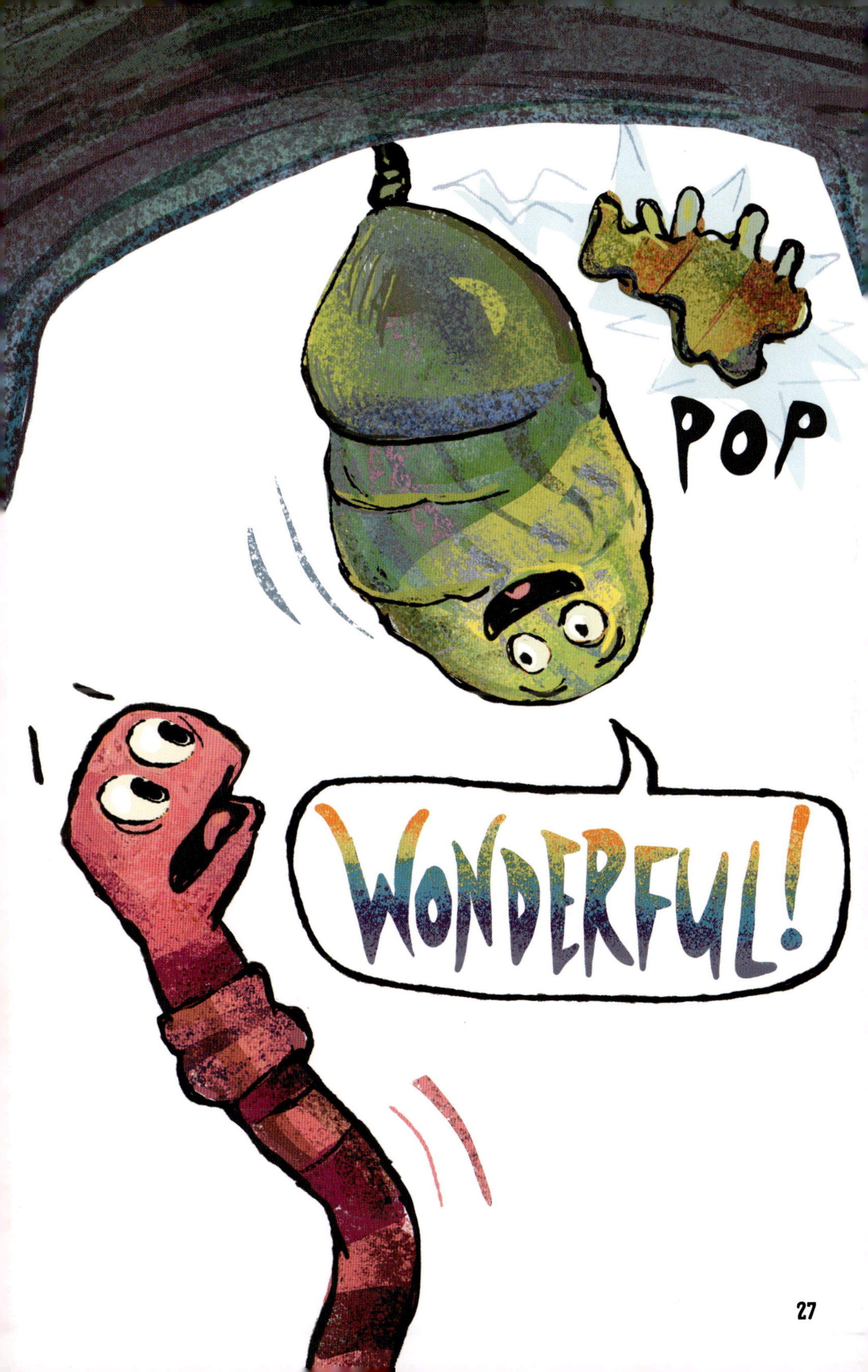
POP
WONDERFUL!

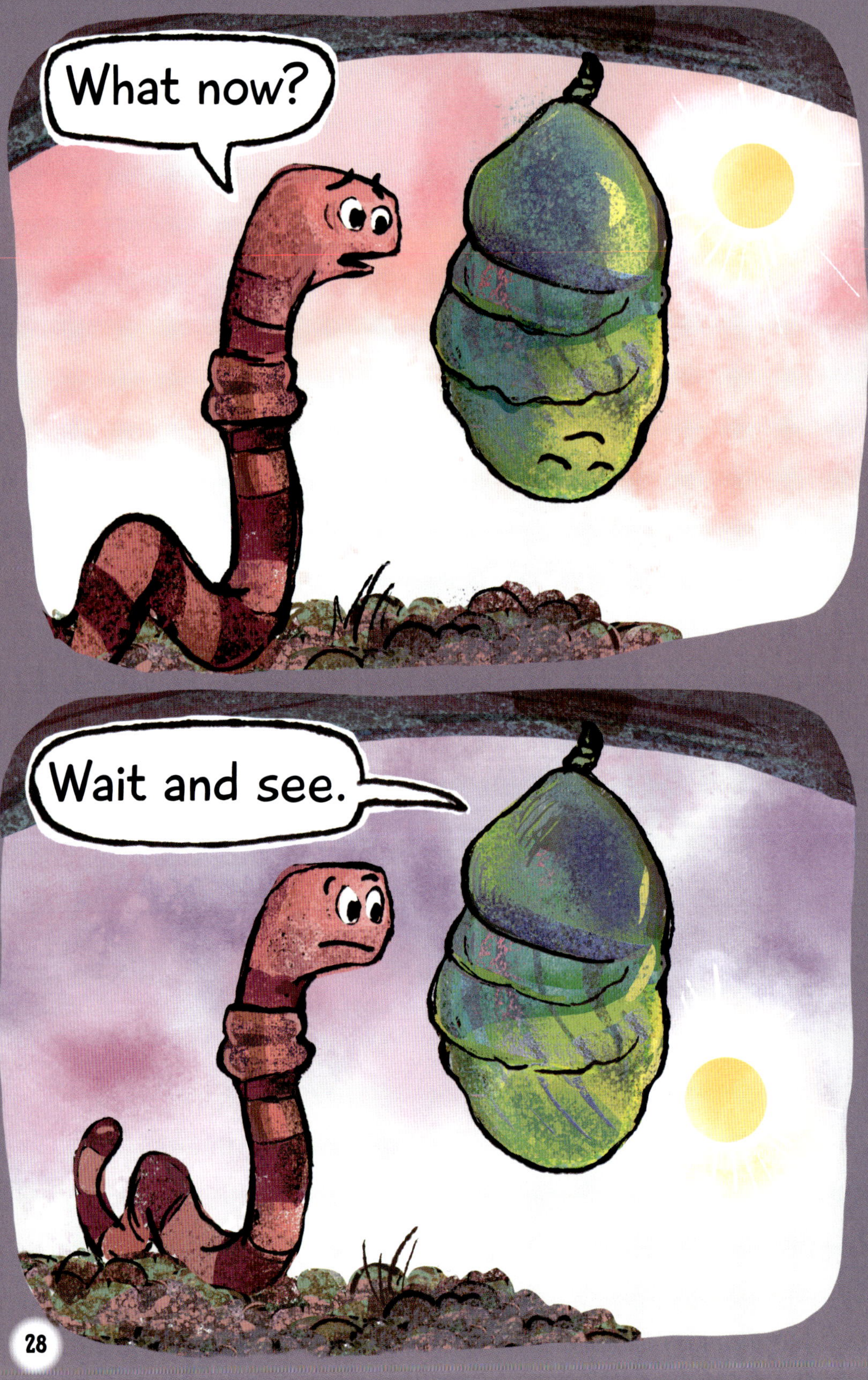
What now?
Wait and see.

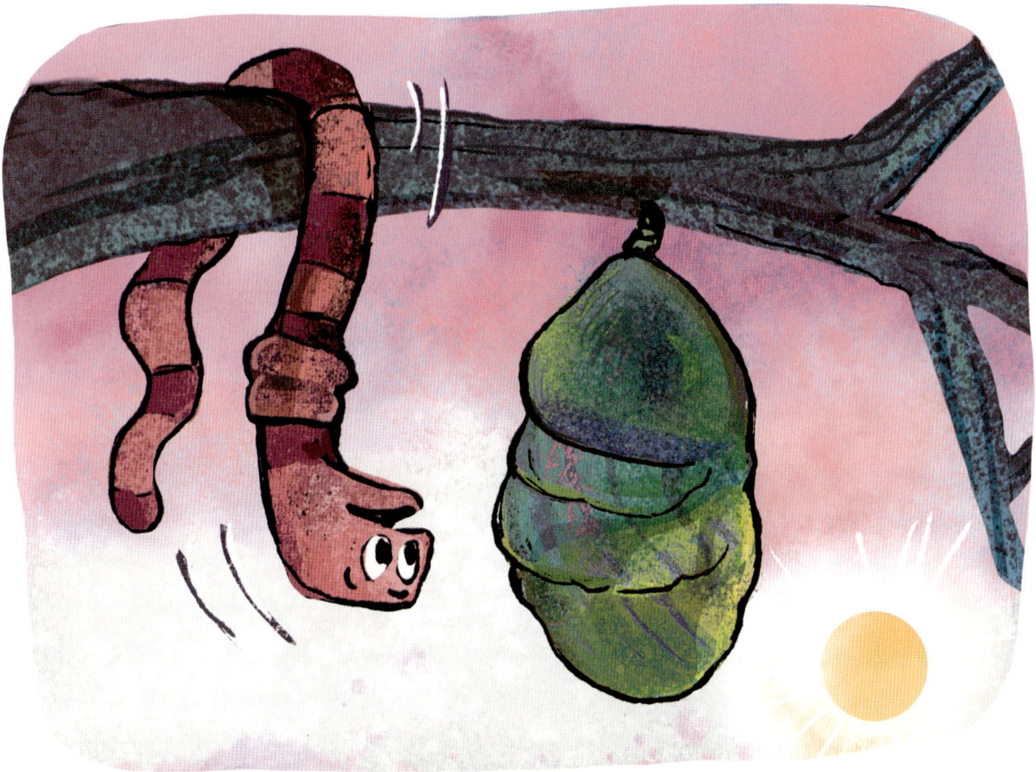

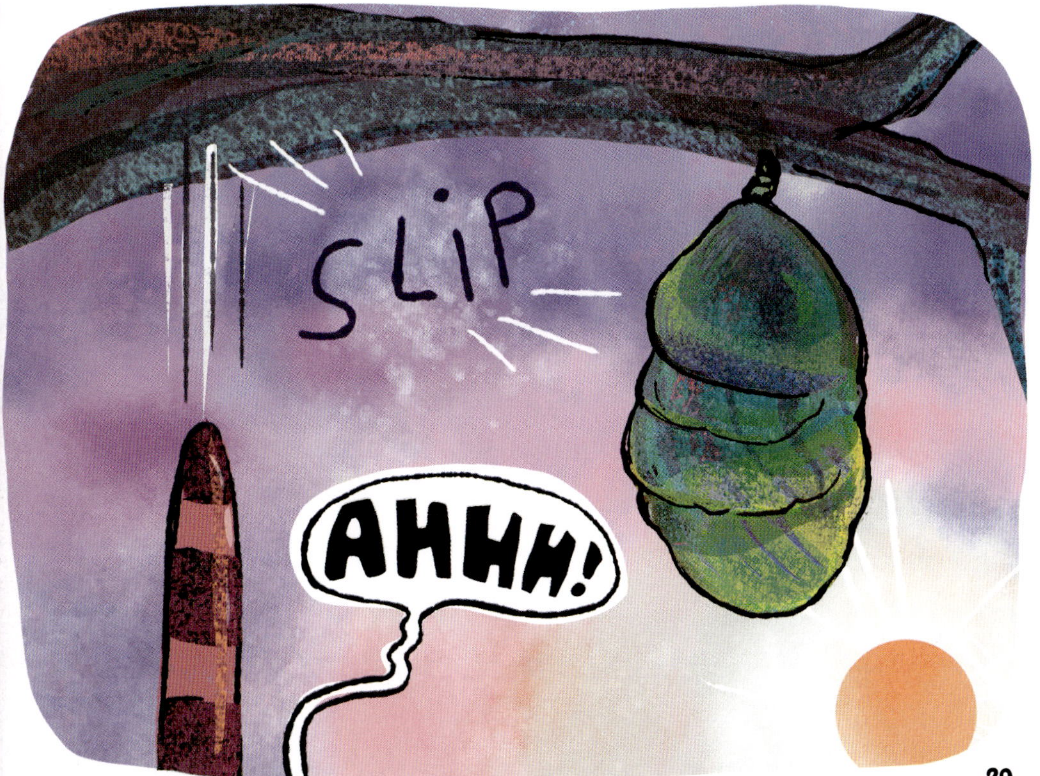
SLIP
AHHH!

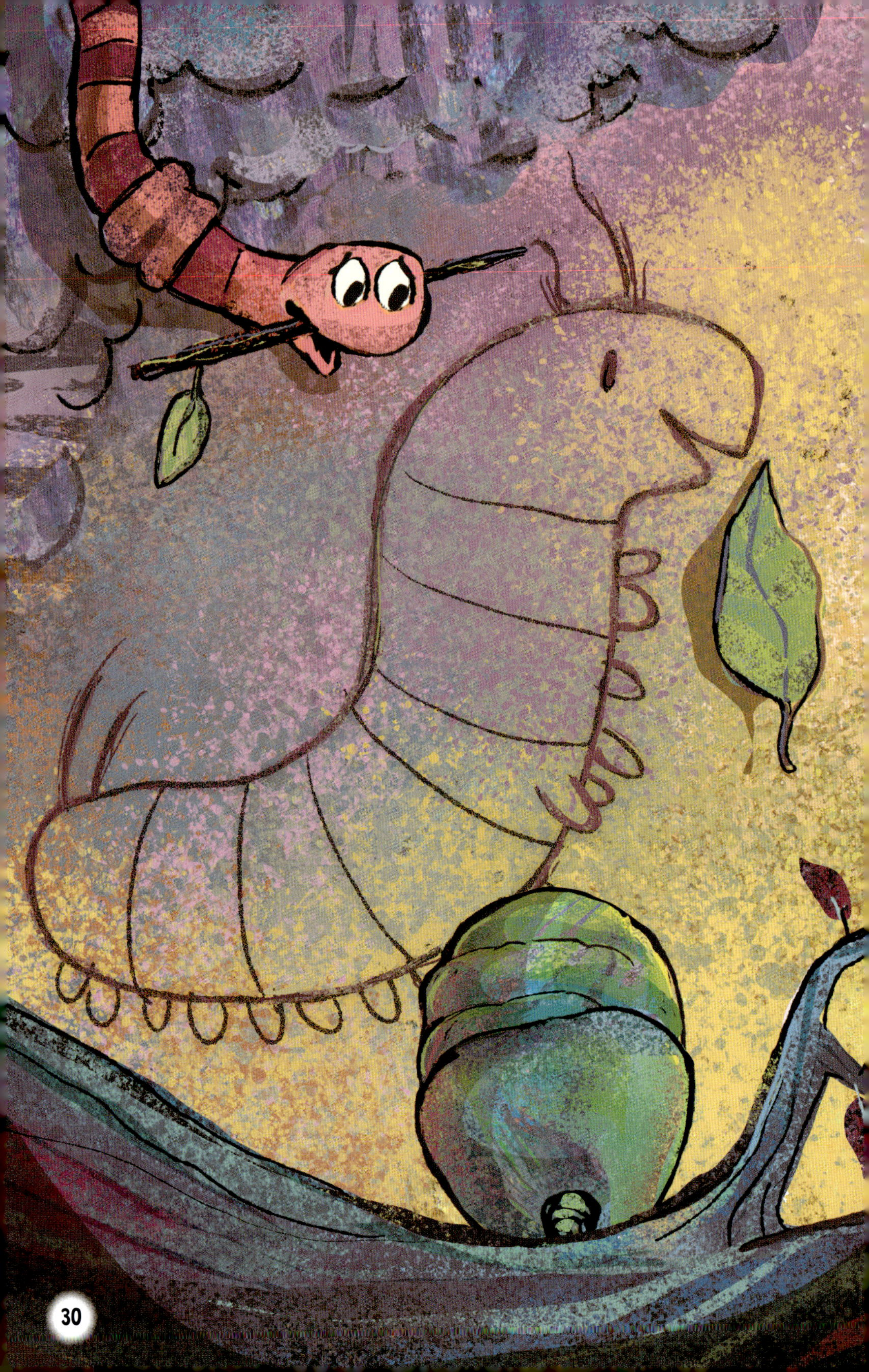

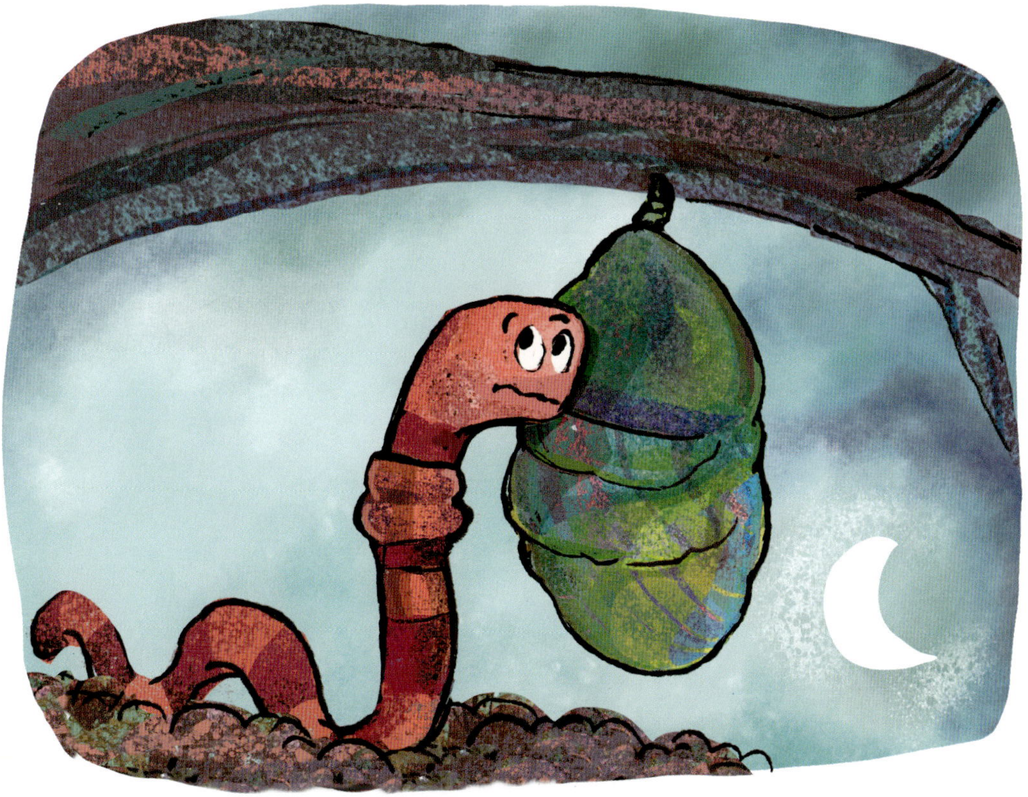

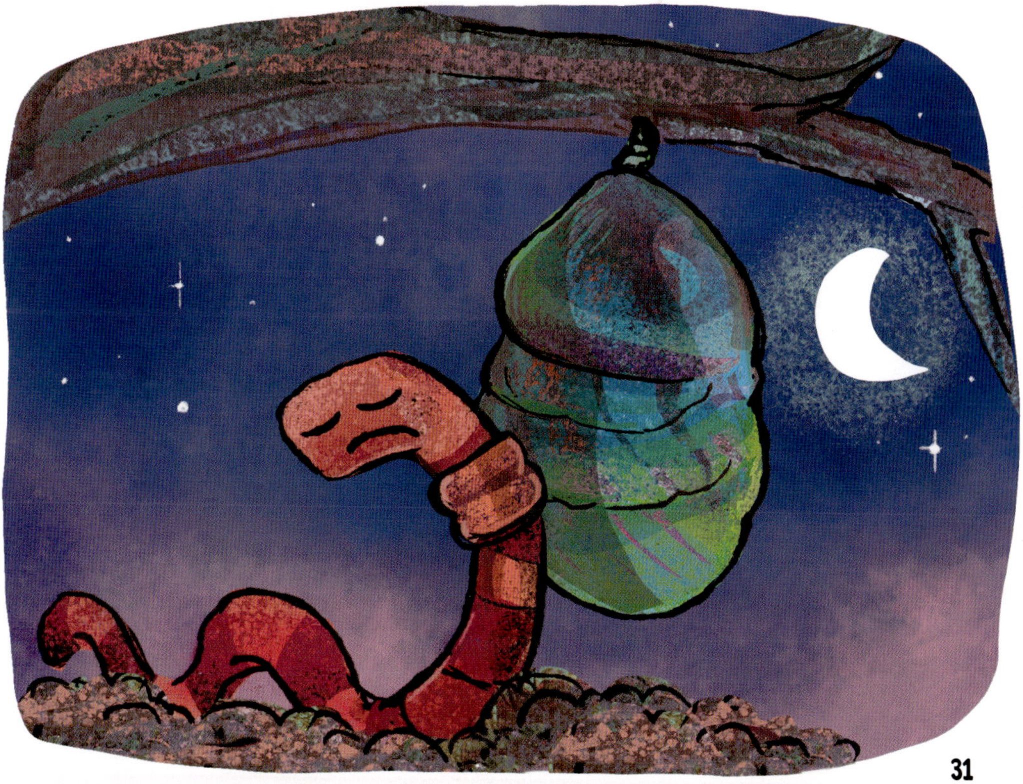

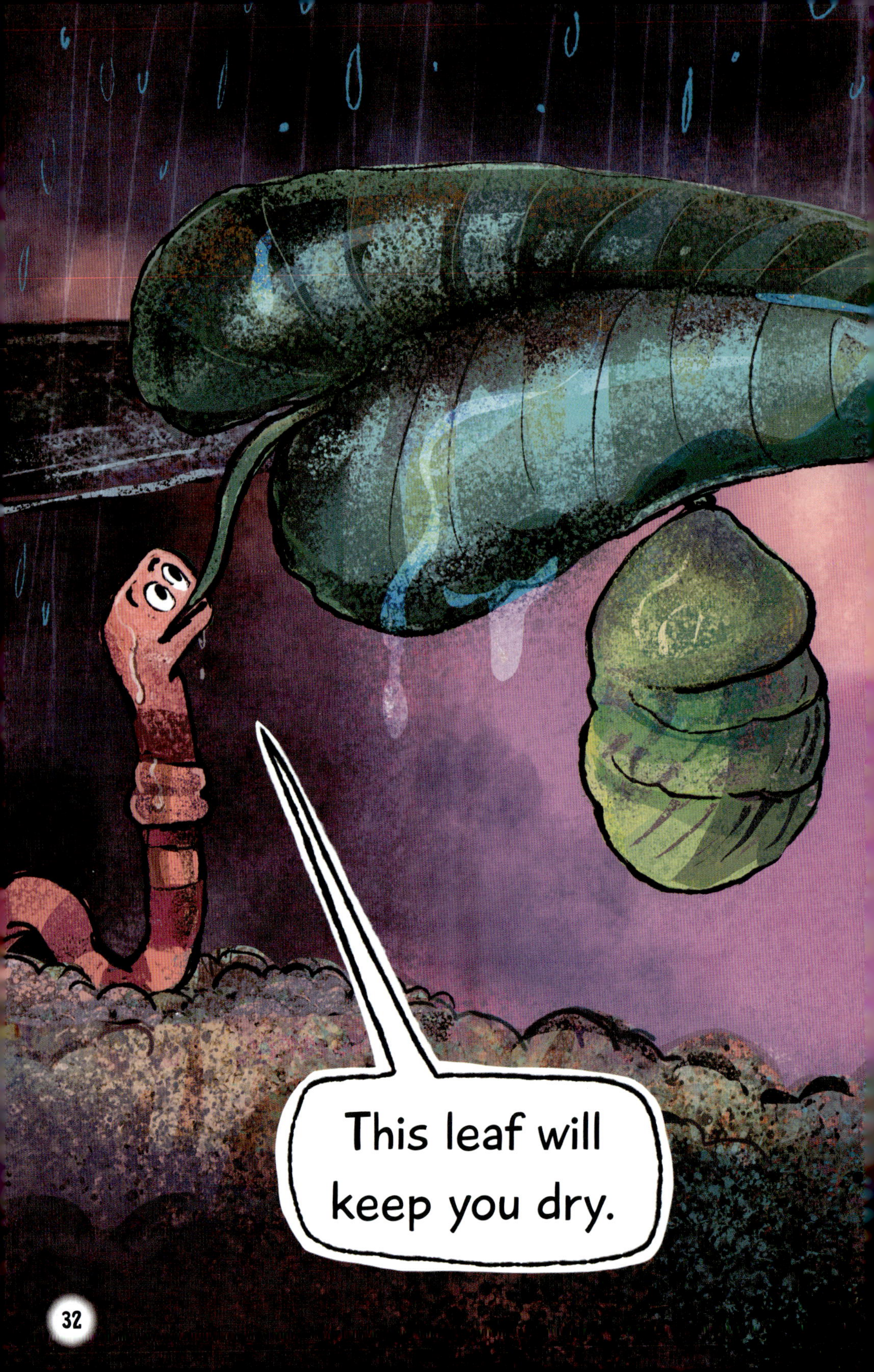
This leaf will keep you dry.

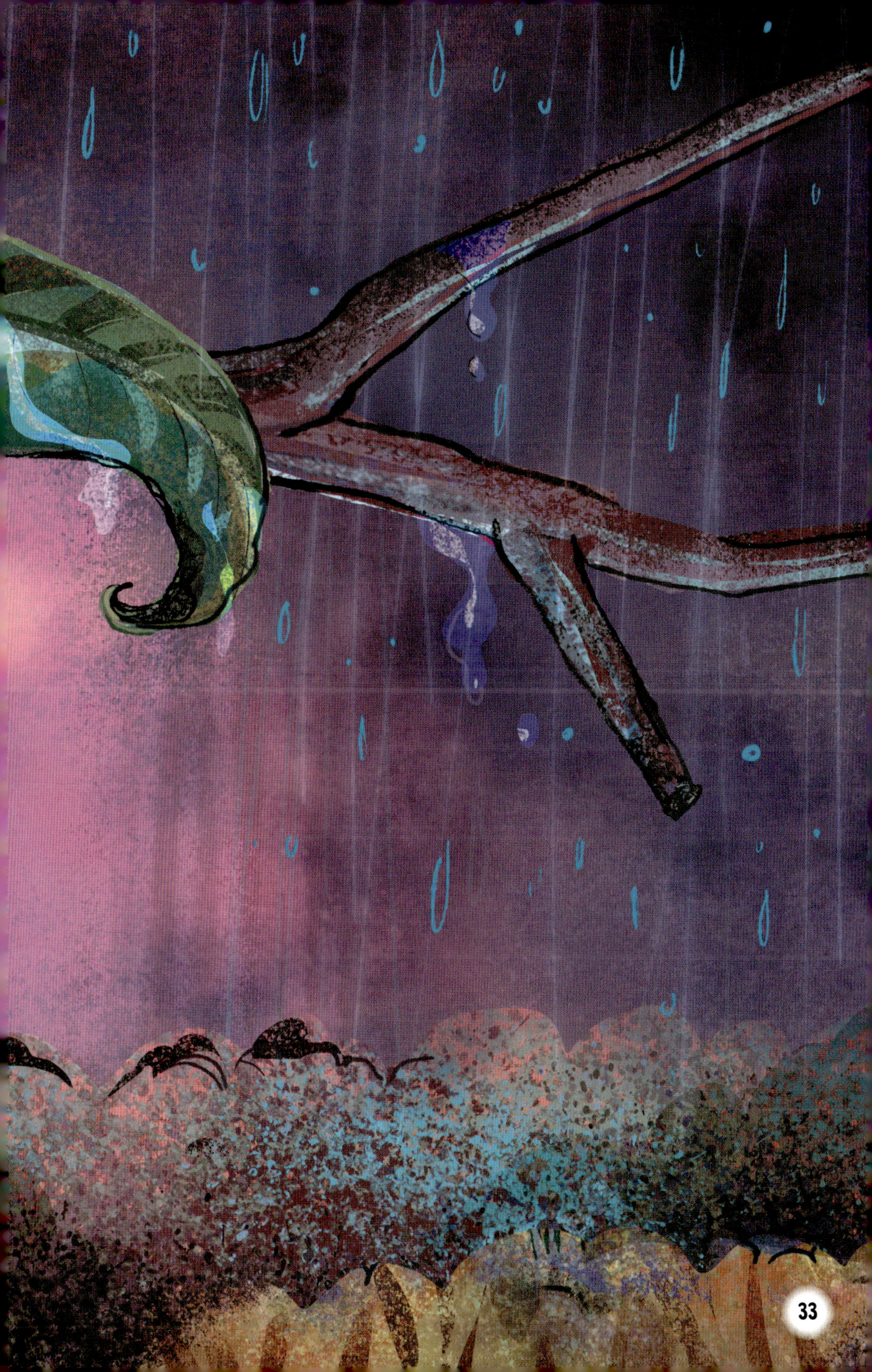

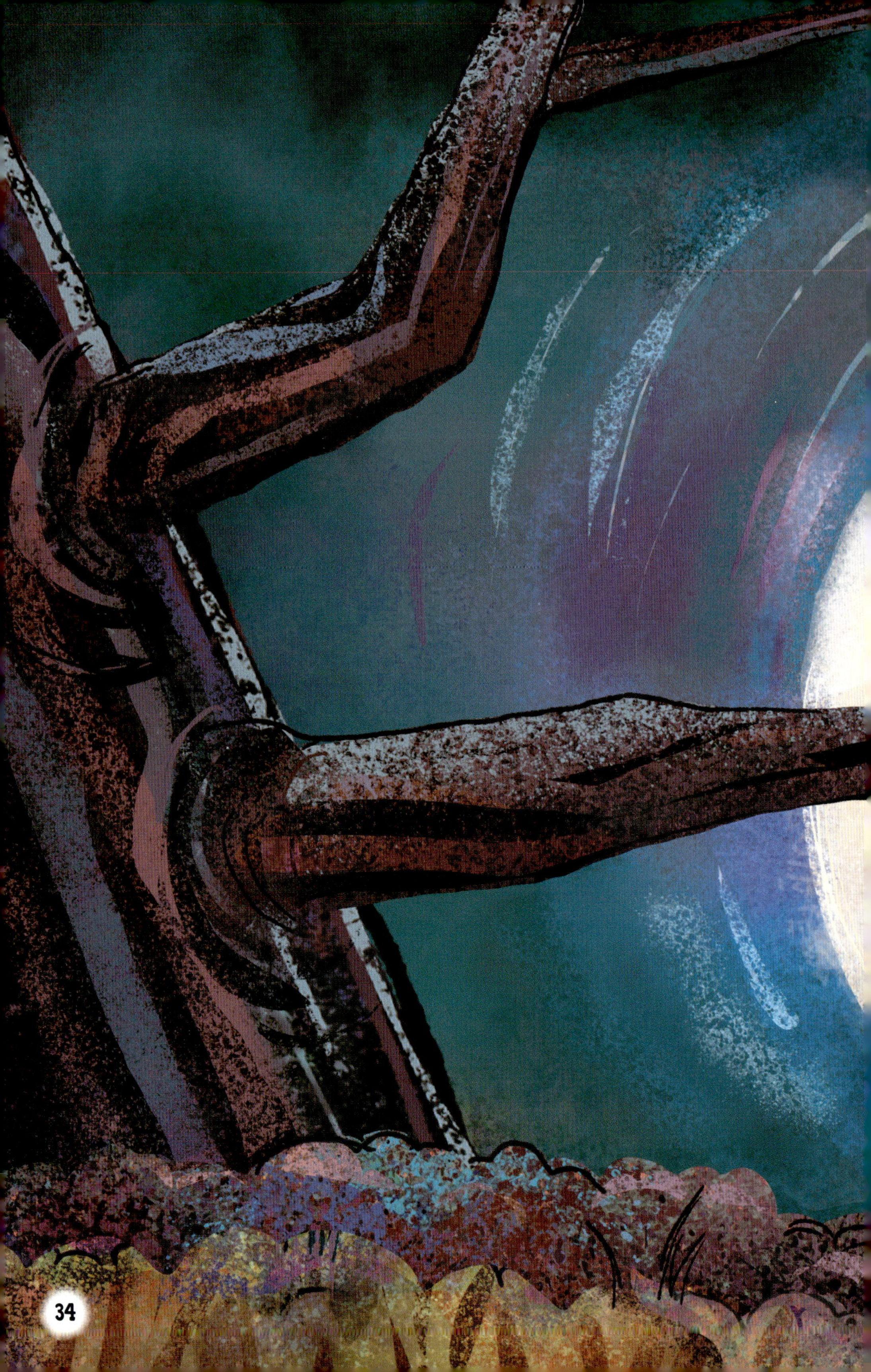

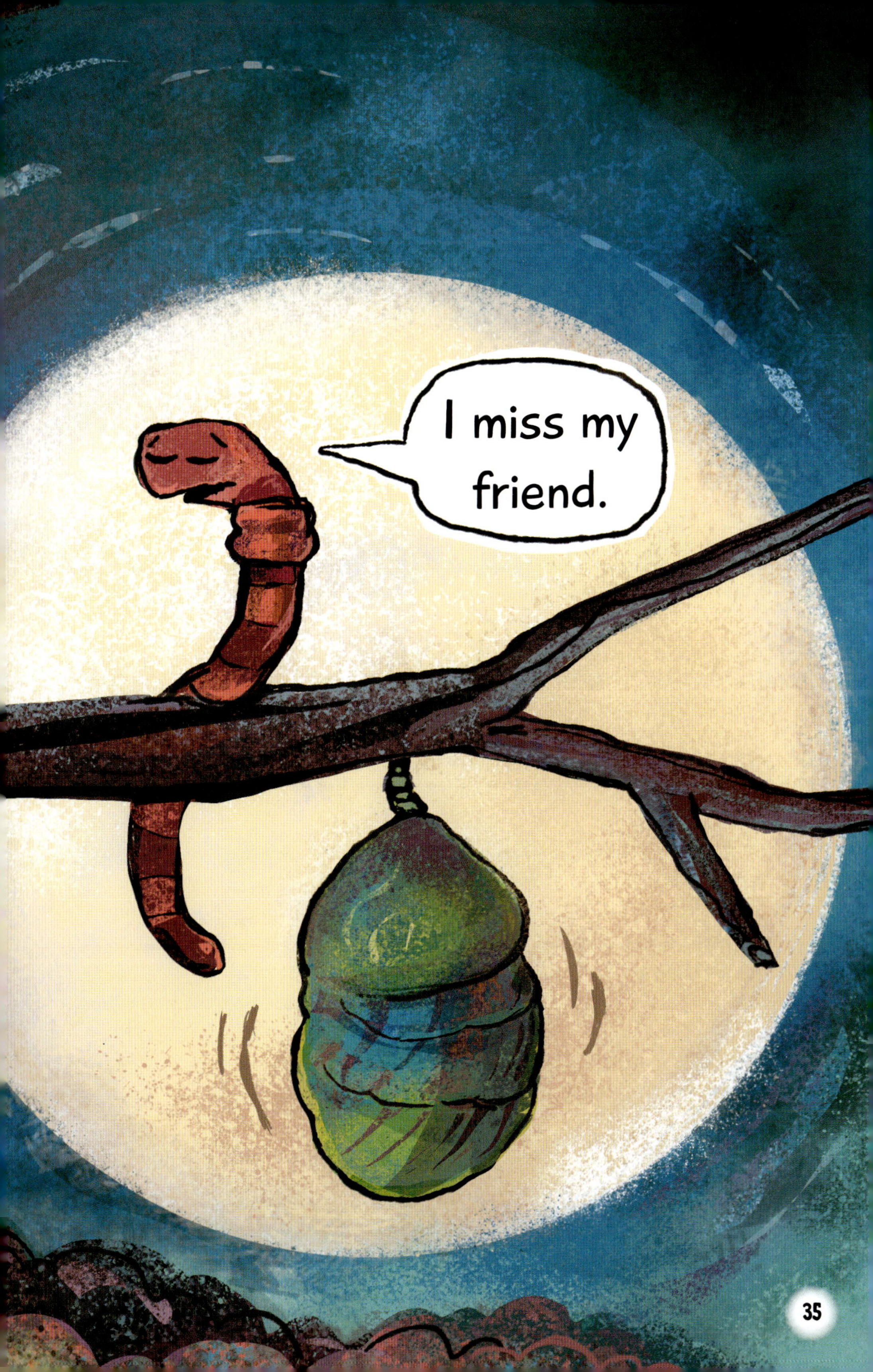
I miss my friend.

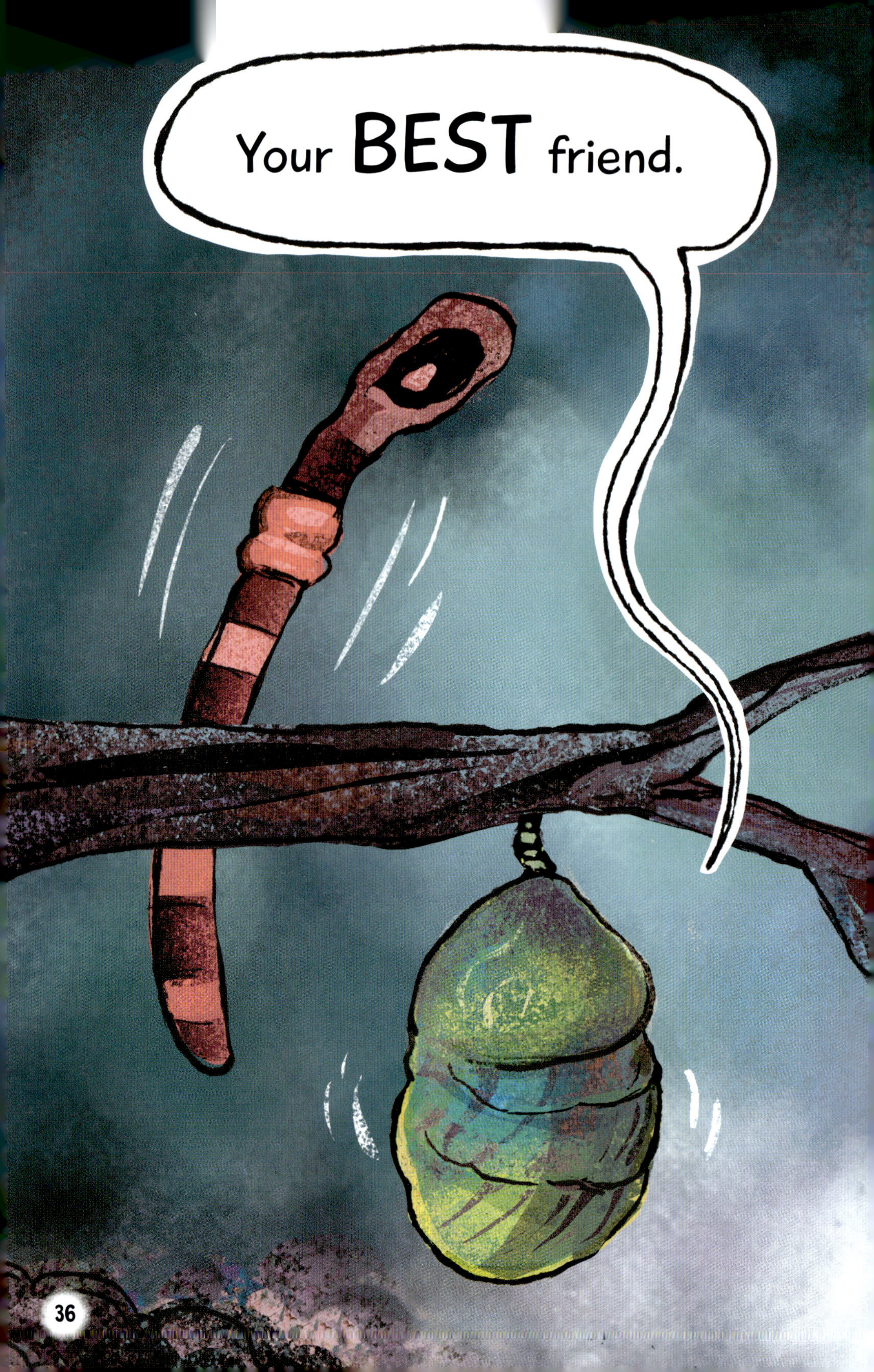
Your BEST friend.

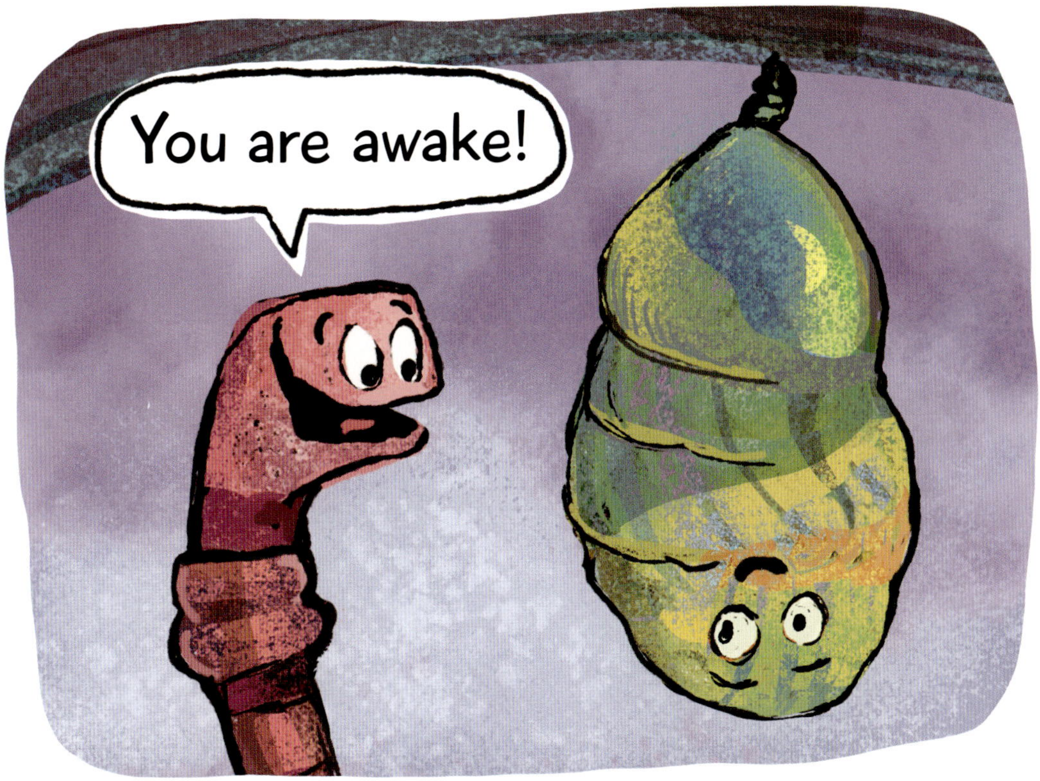
You are awake!

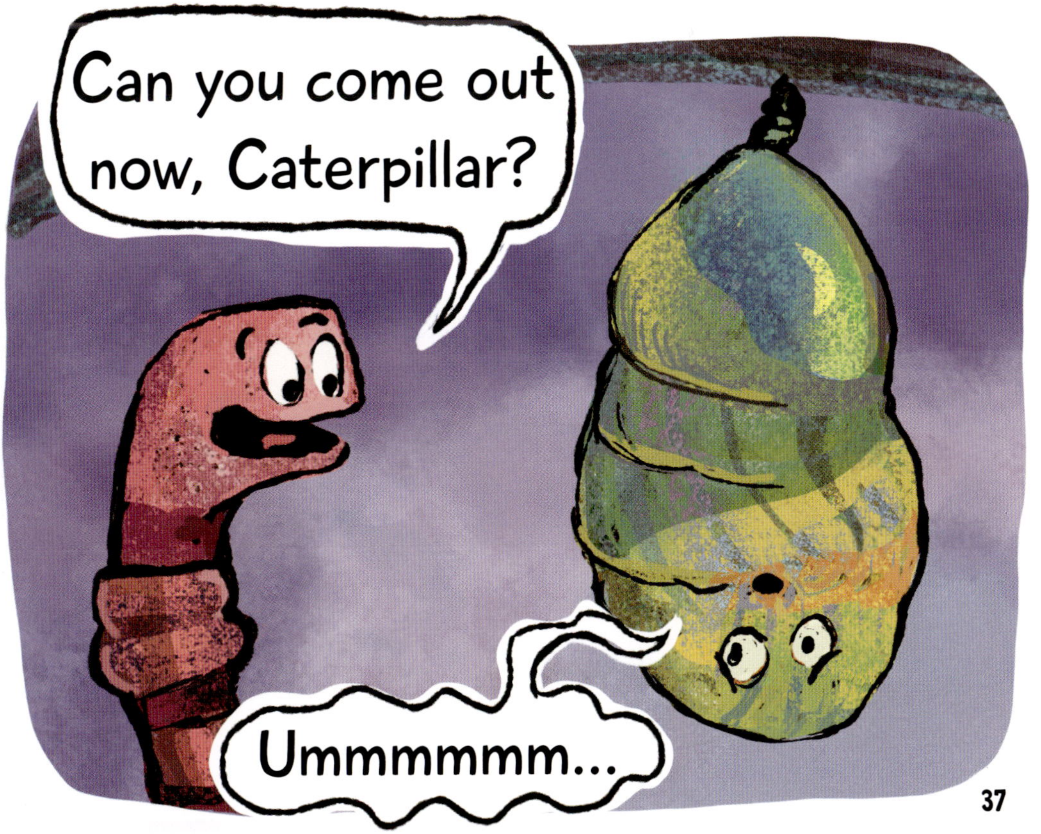
Can you come out now, Caterpillar?
Ummmmmm...

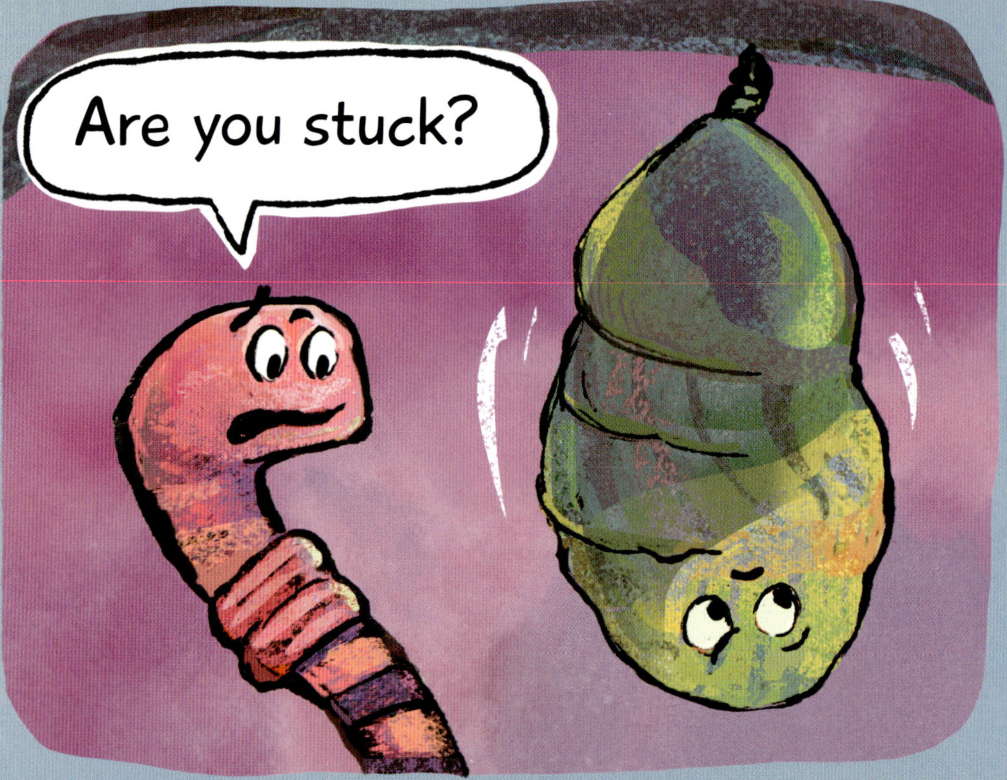
Are you stuck?

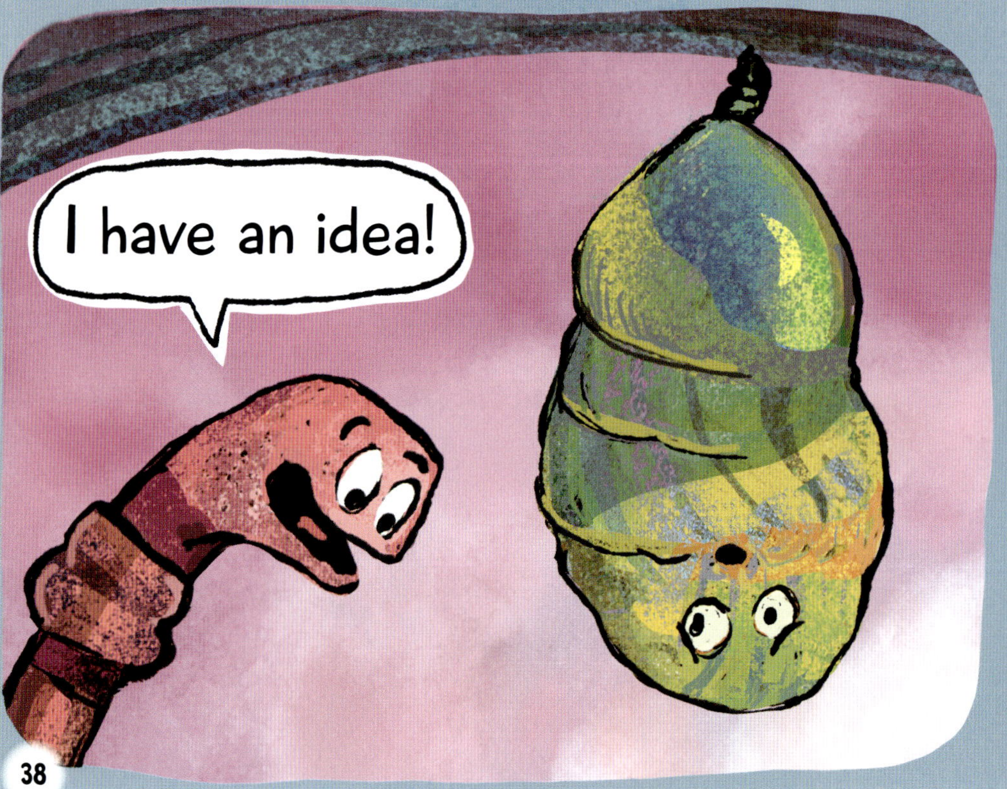
I have an idea!

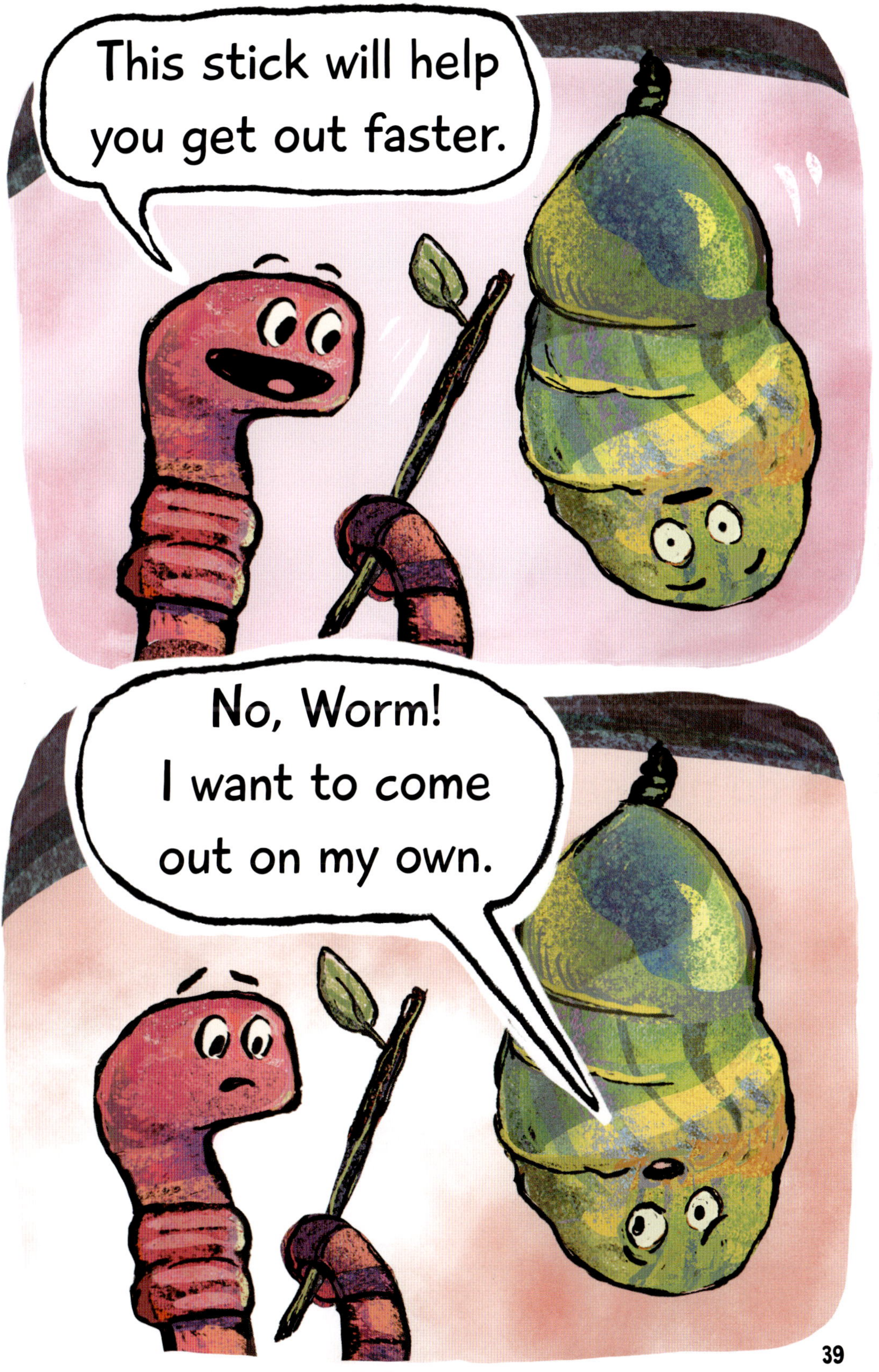
This stick will help you get out faster.
No, Worm! I want to come out on my own.

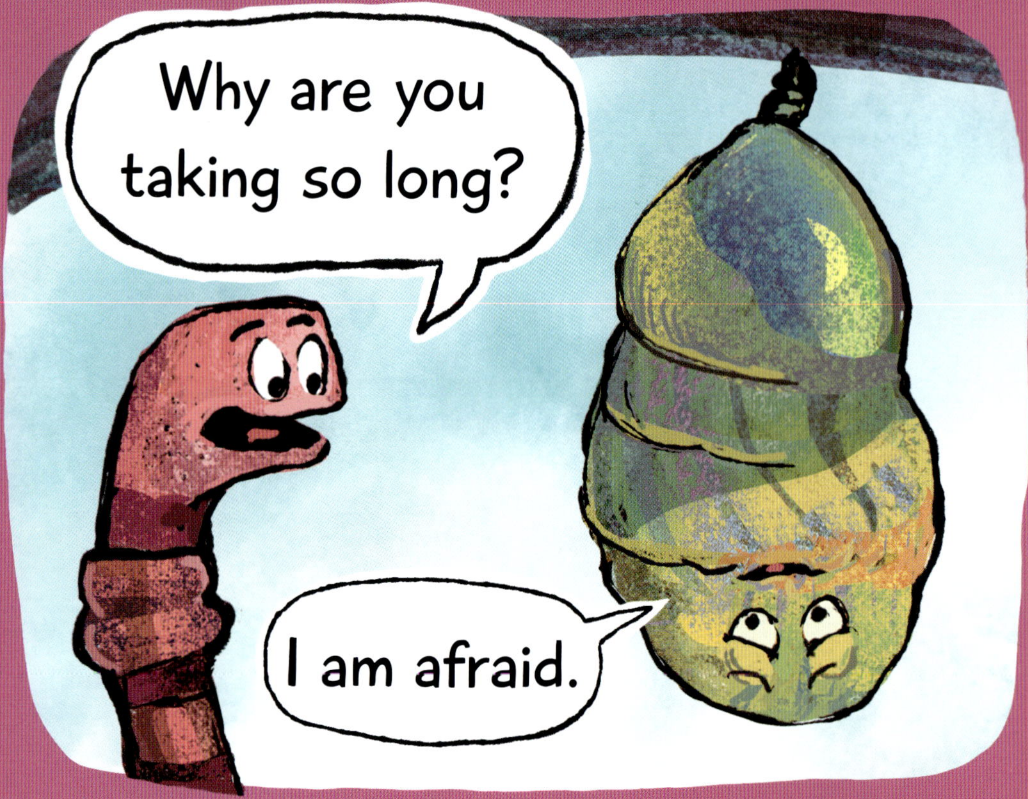
Why are you taking so long?
I am afraid.

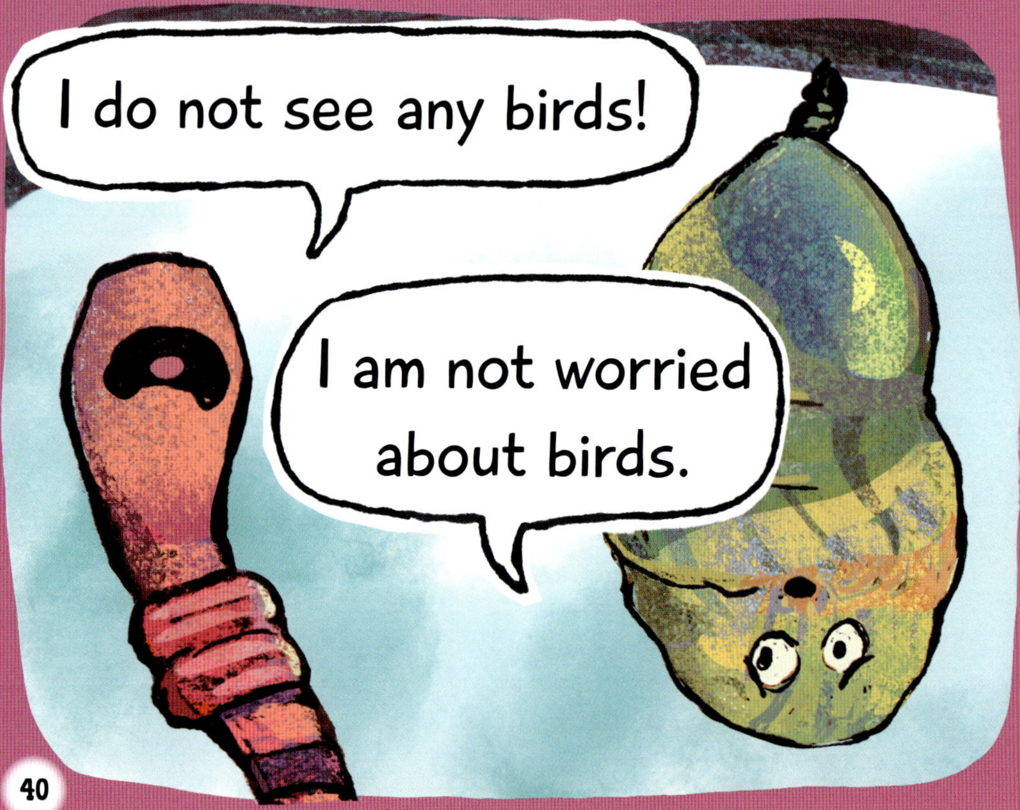
I do not see any birds!
I am not worried about birds.

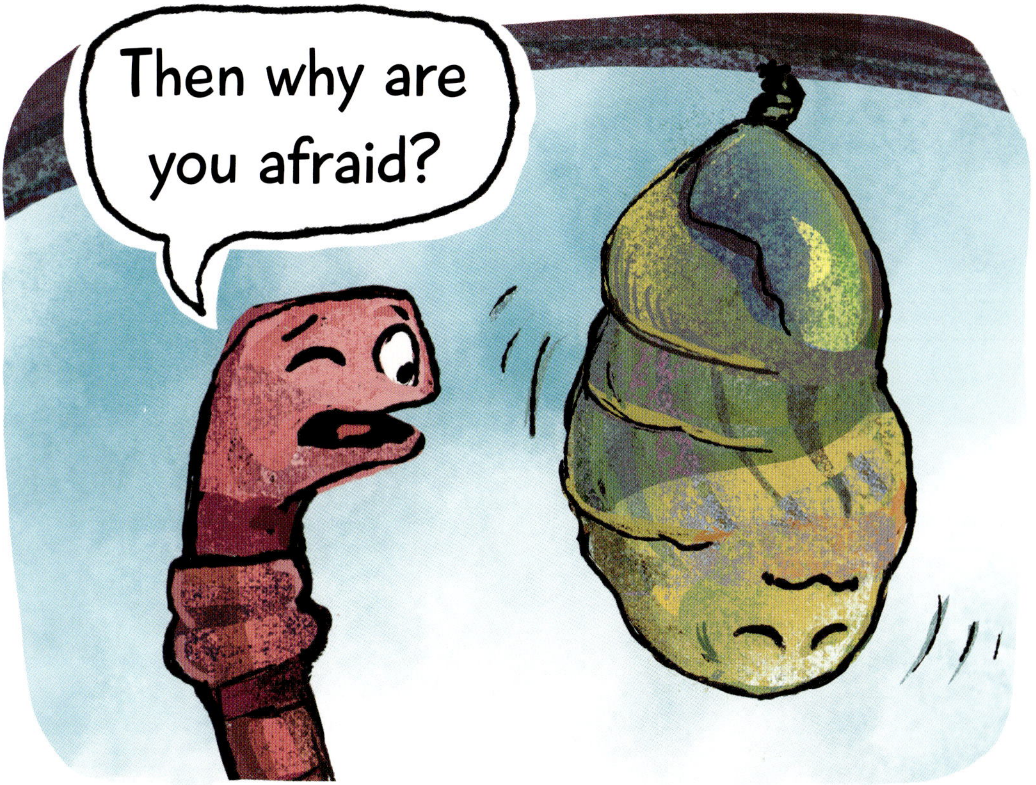
Then why are you afraid?

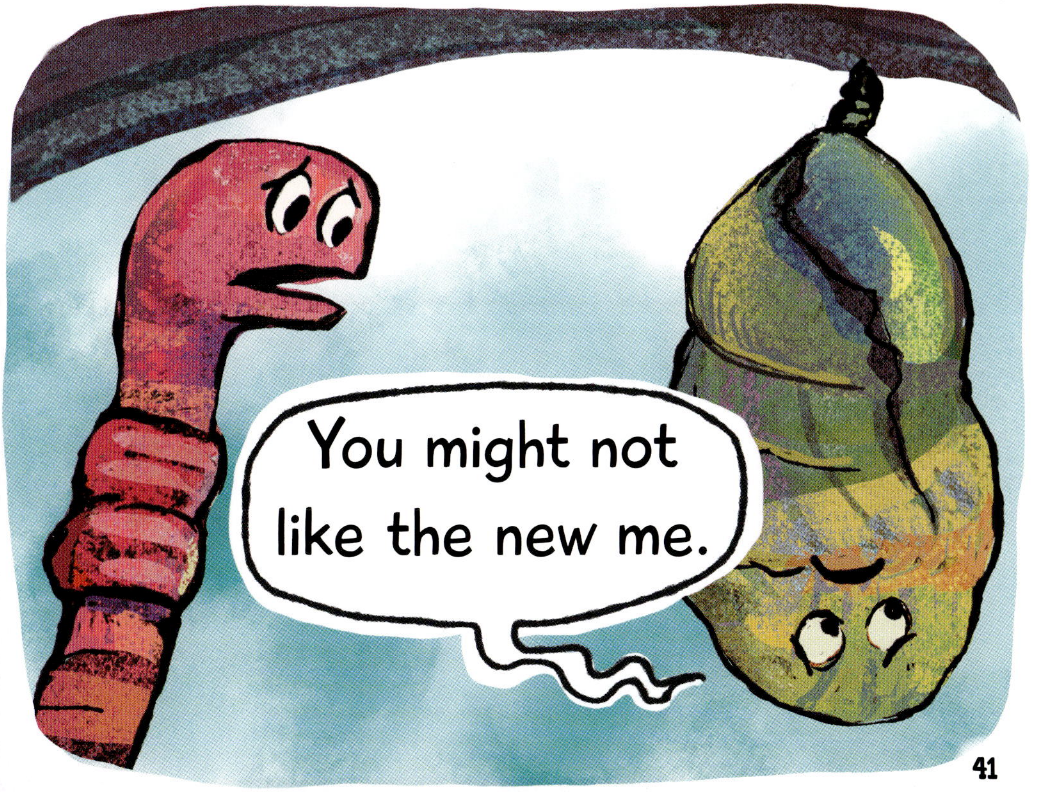
You might not like the new me.

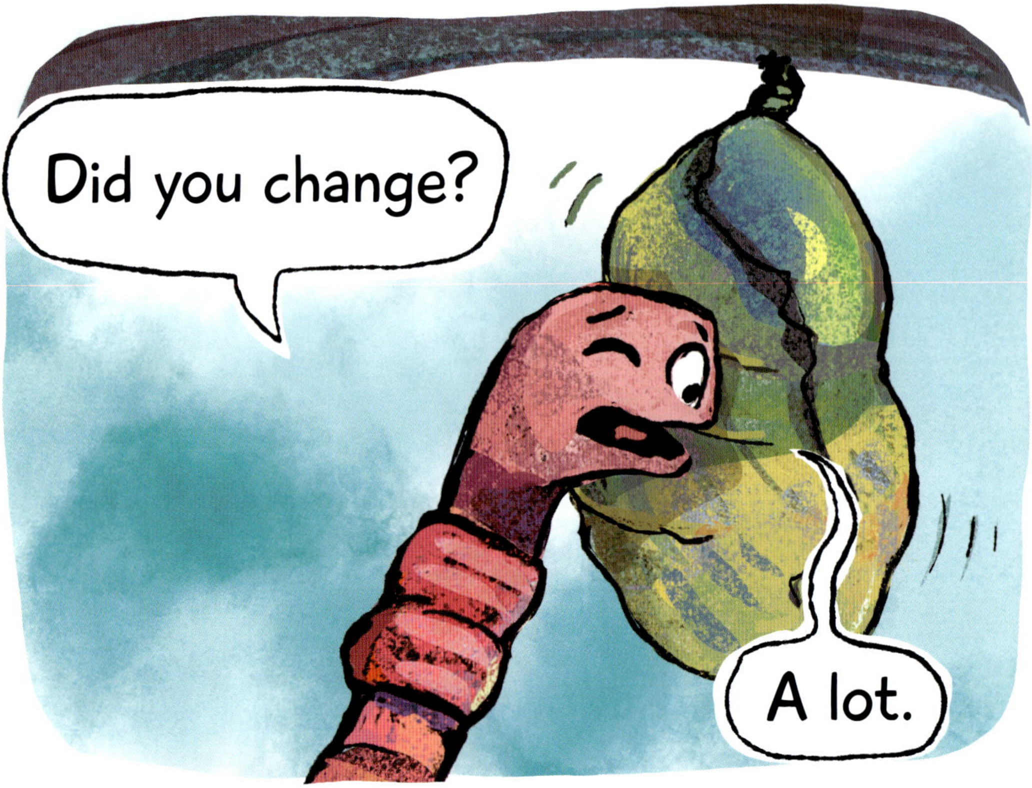
Did you change?
A lot.

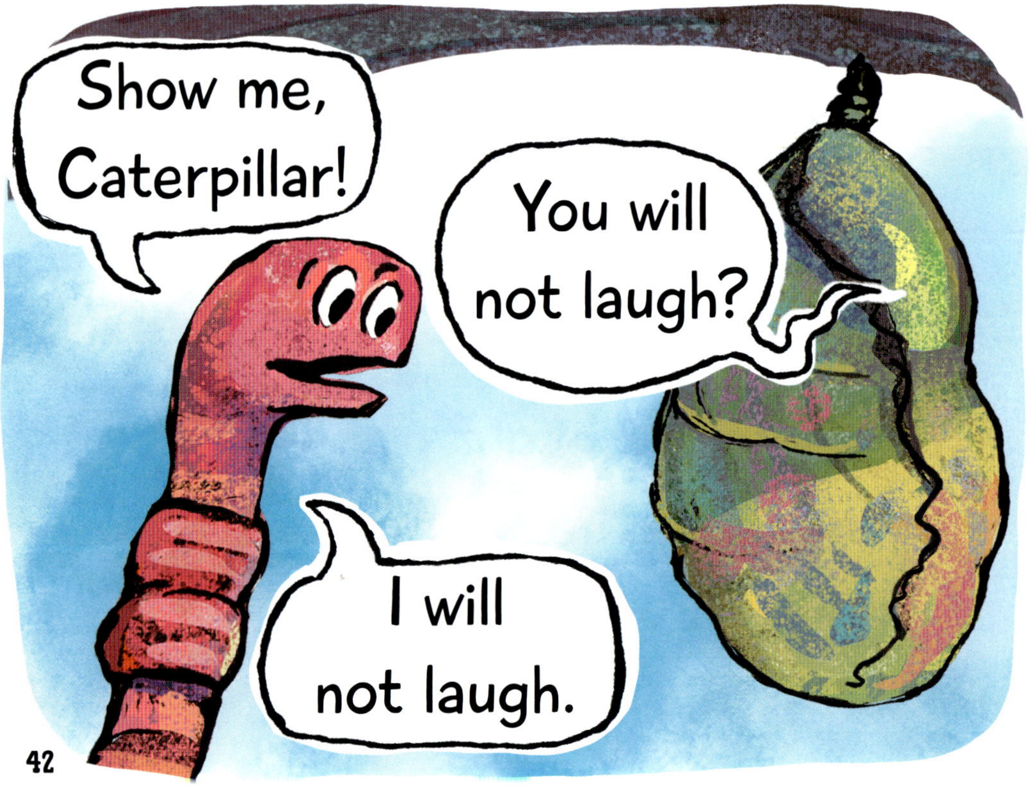
Show me, Caterpillar!
You will not laugh?
I will not laugh.

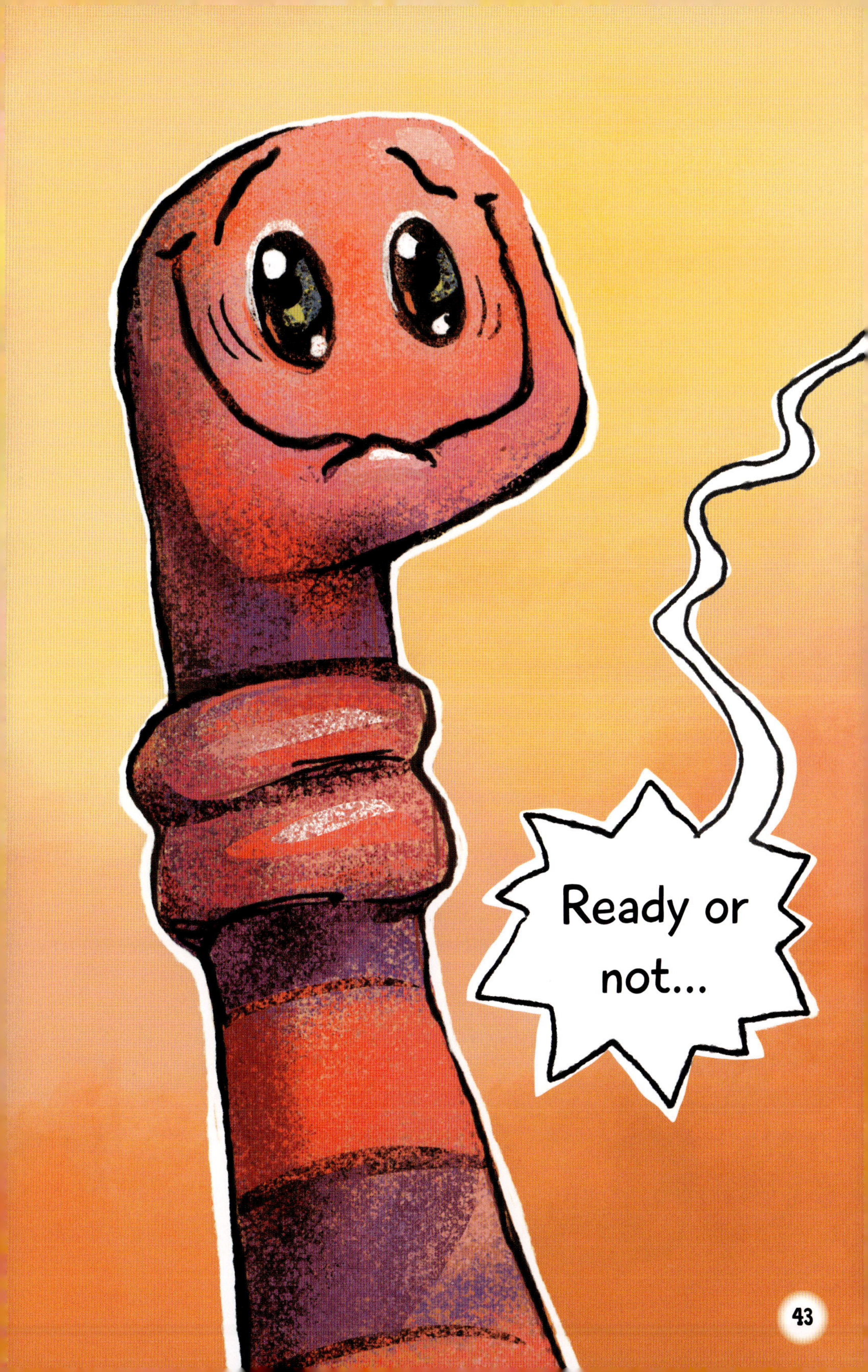
Ready or not...

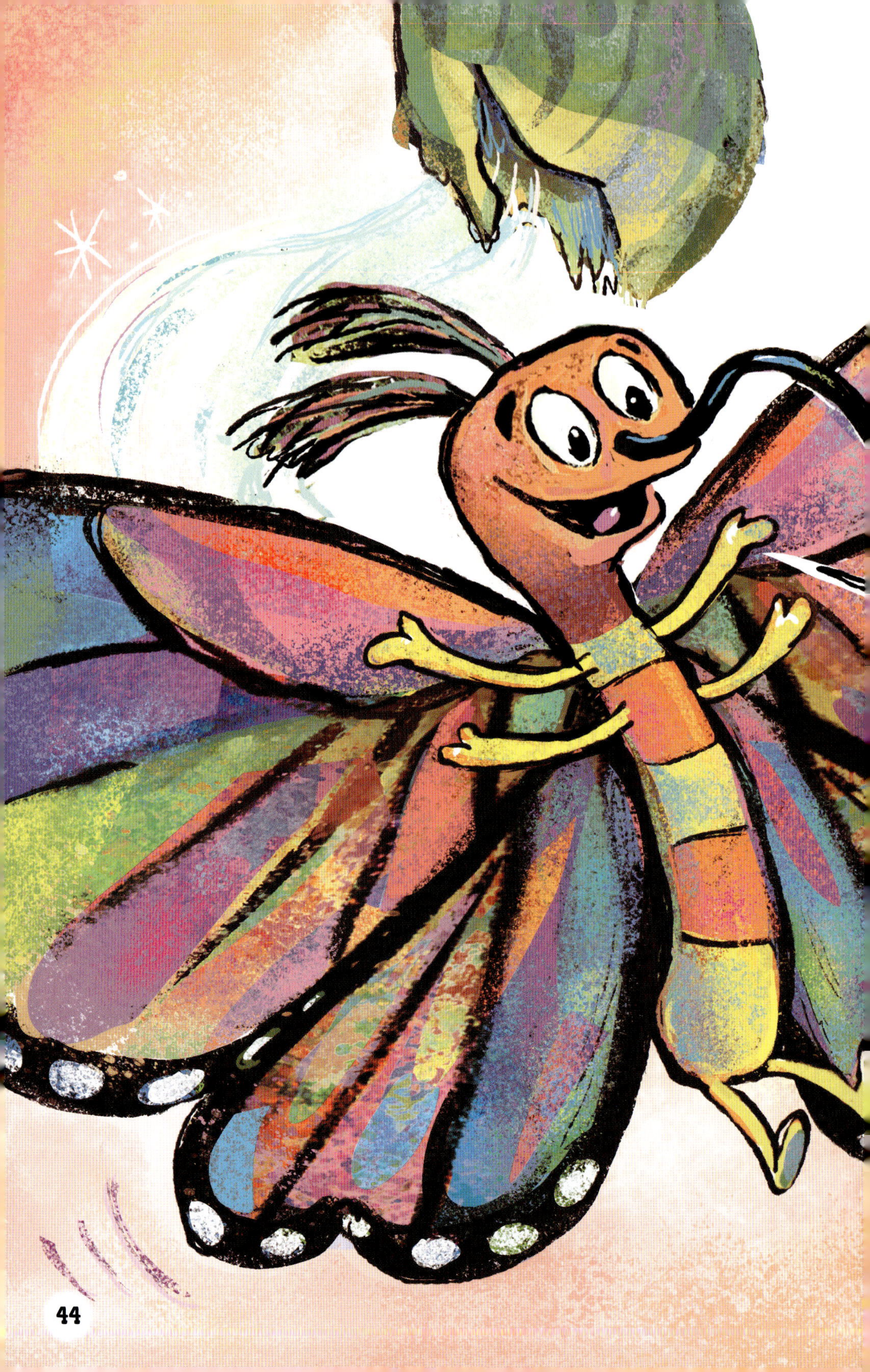

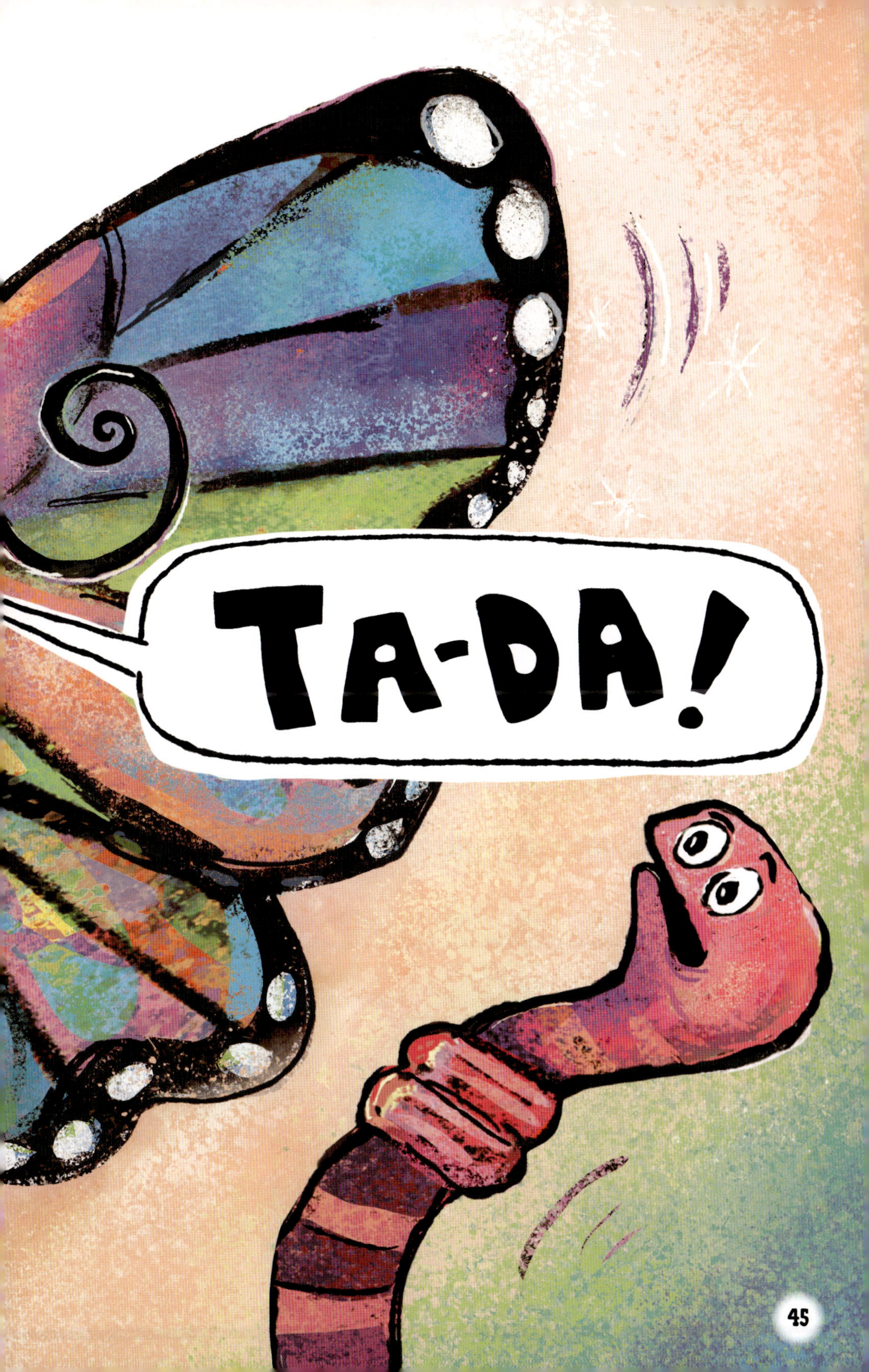
TA-DA!

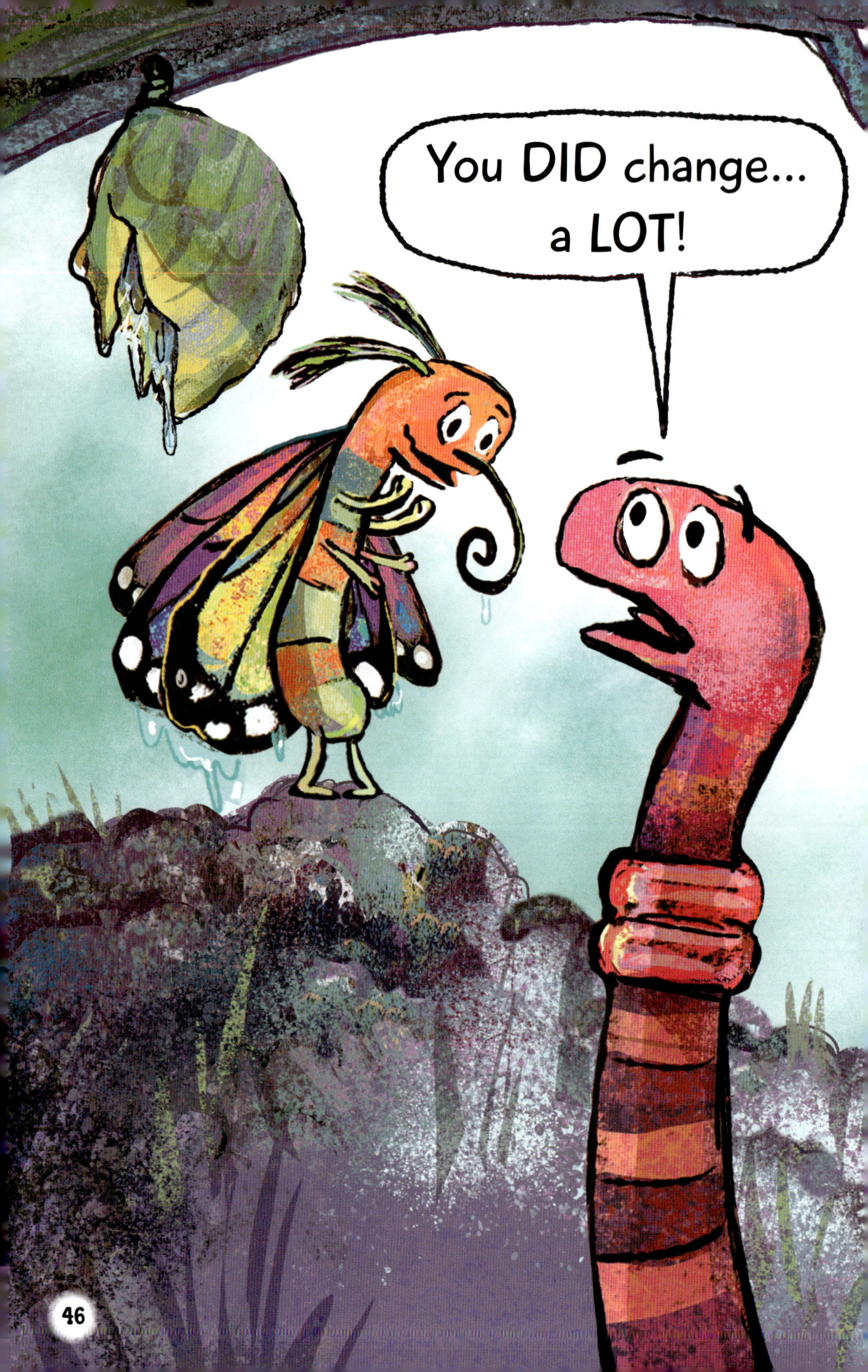
You DID change...
a LOT!

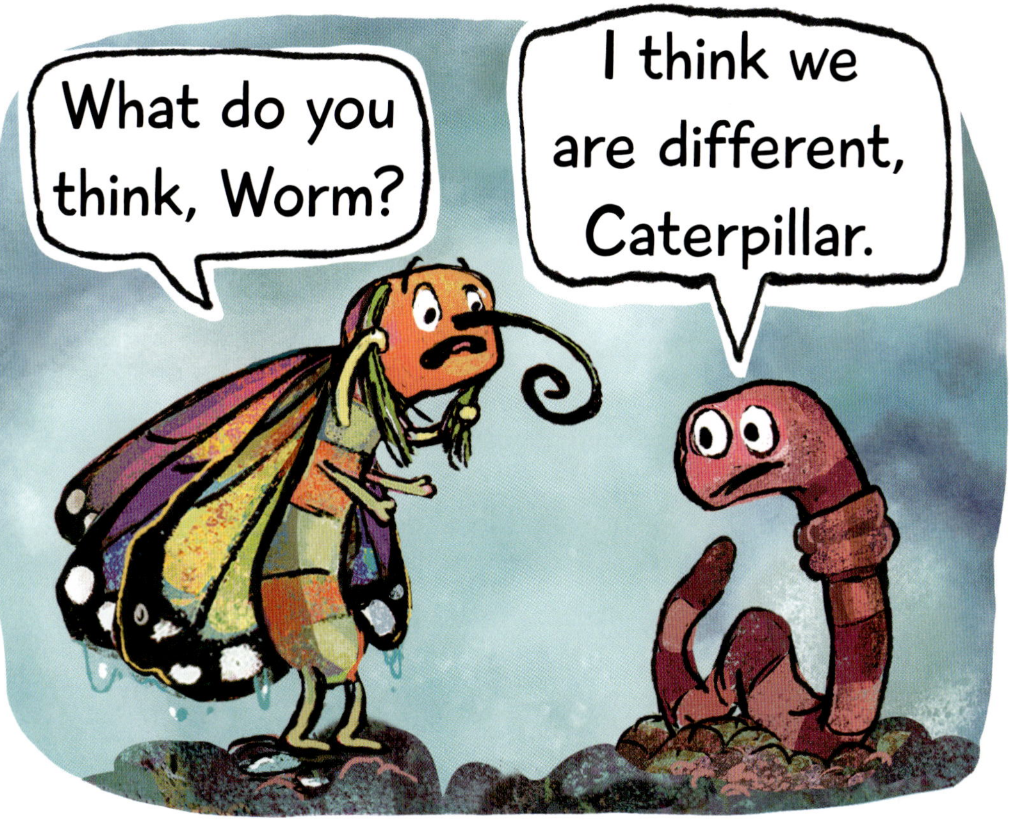
What do you think, Worm?
I think we are different, Caterpillar.

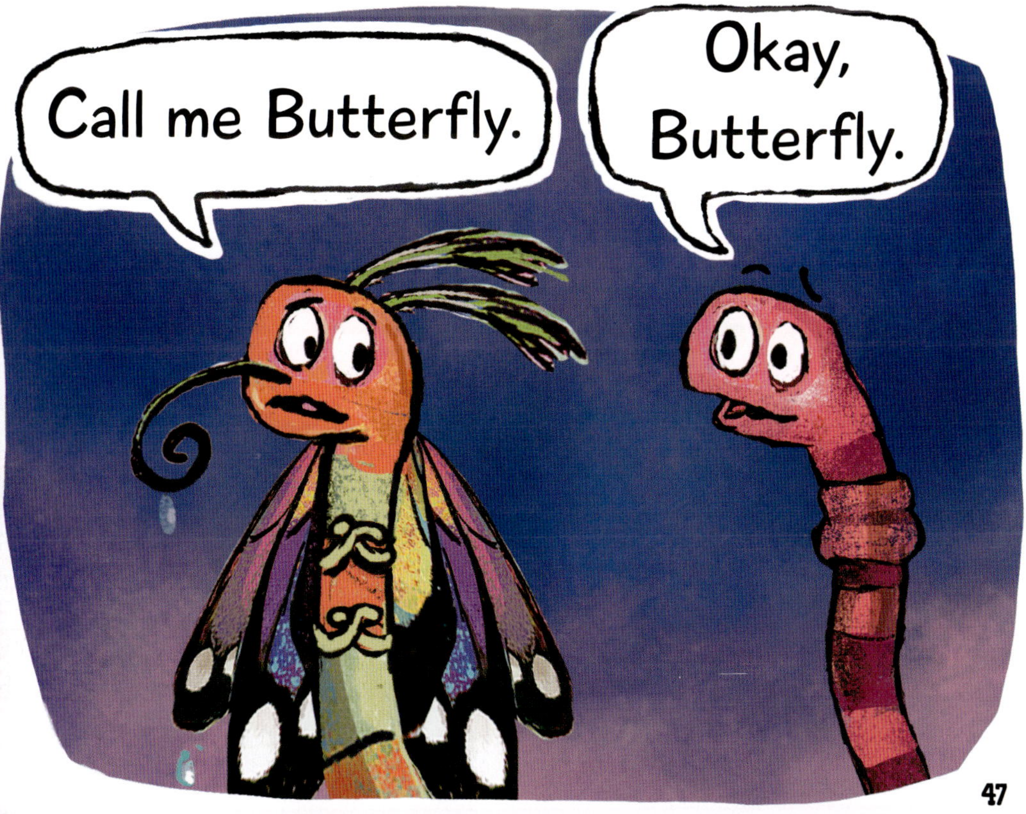
Call me Butterfly.
Okay, Butterfly.

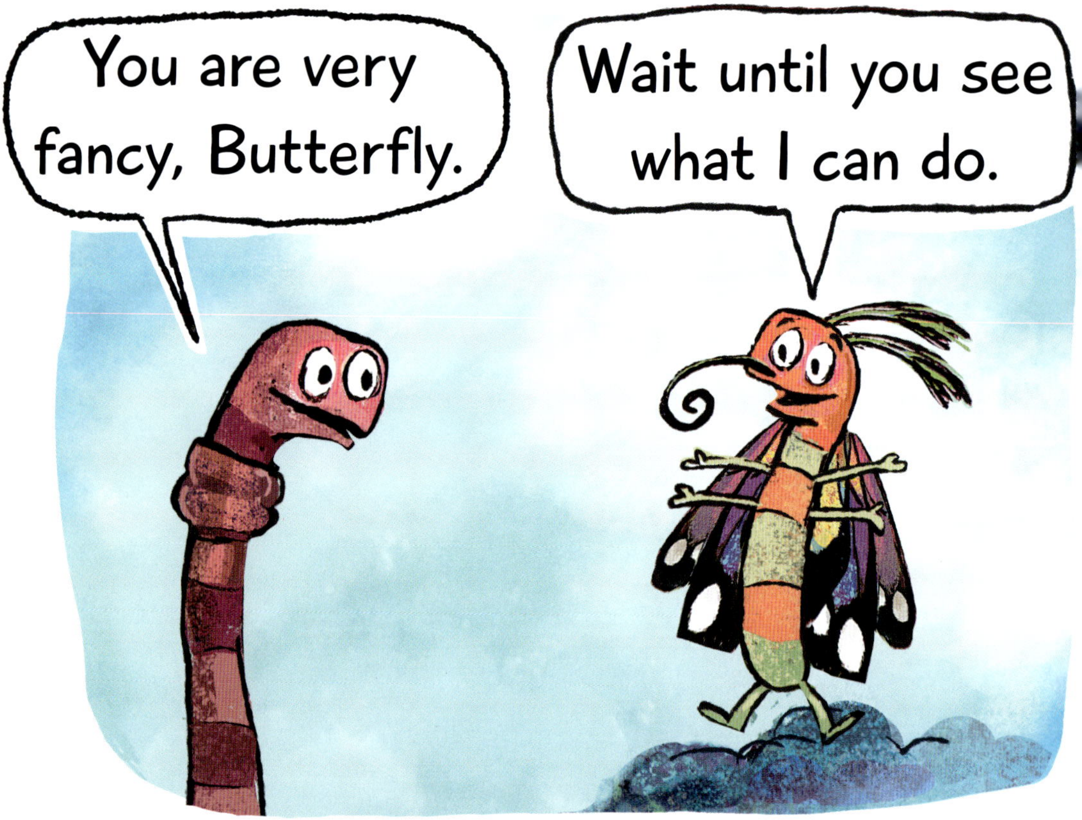
You are very fancy, Butterfly.
Wait until you see what I can do.

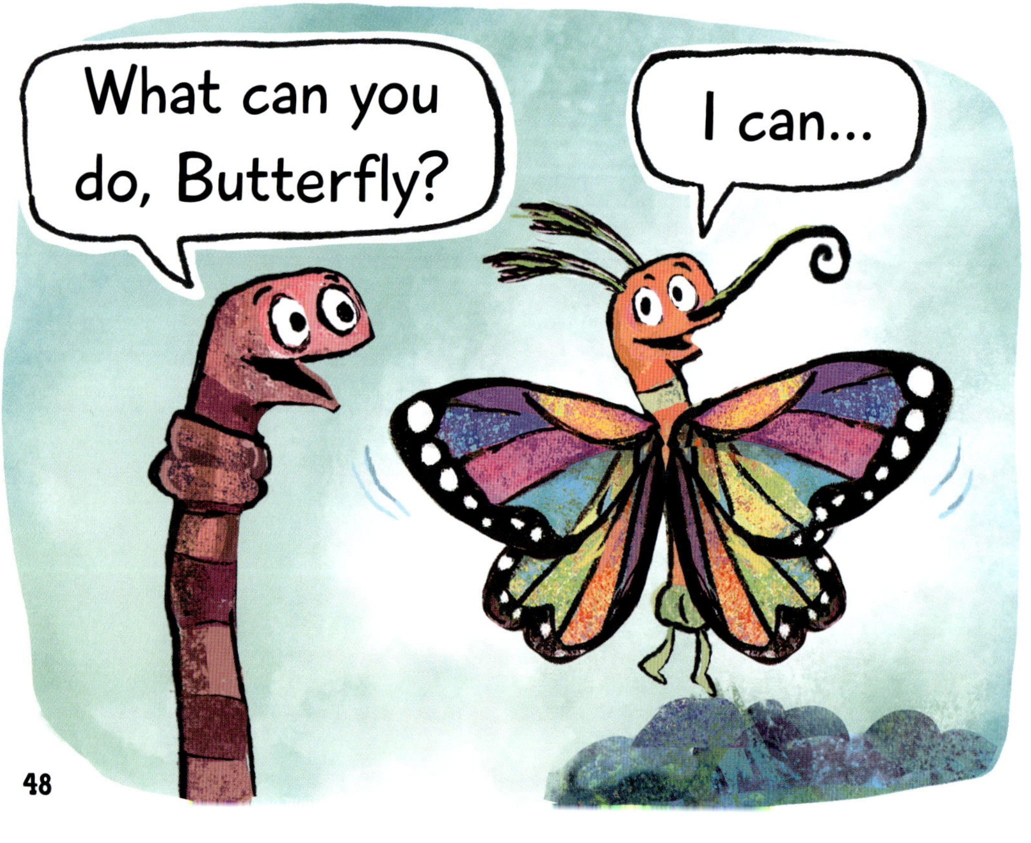
What can you do, Butterfly?
I can...

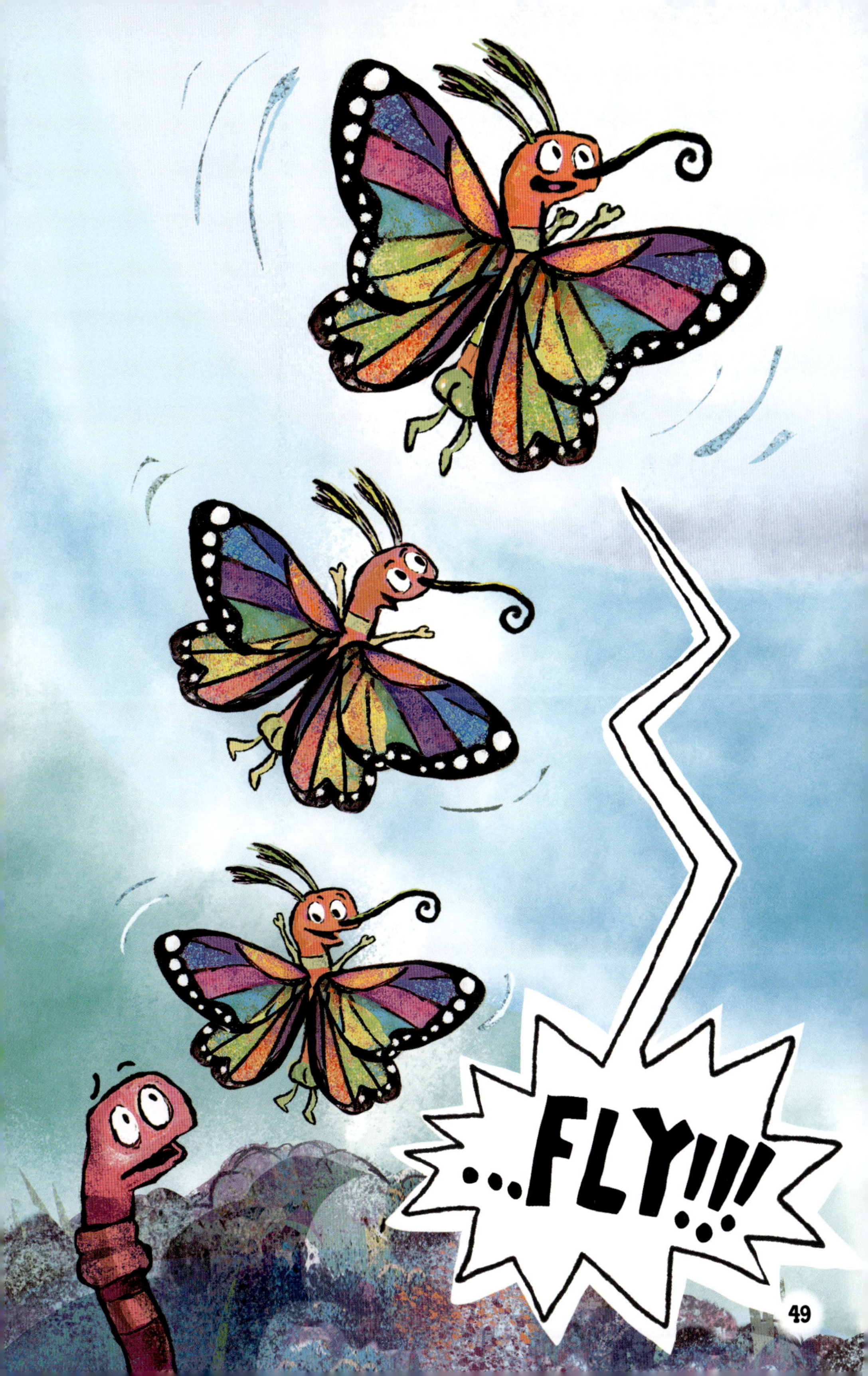
...FLY!!!

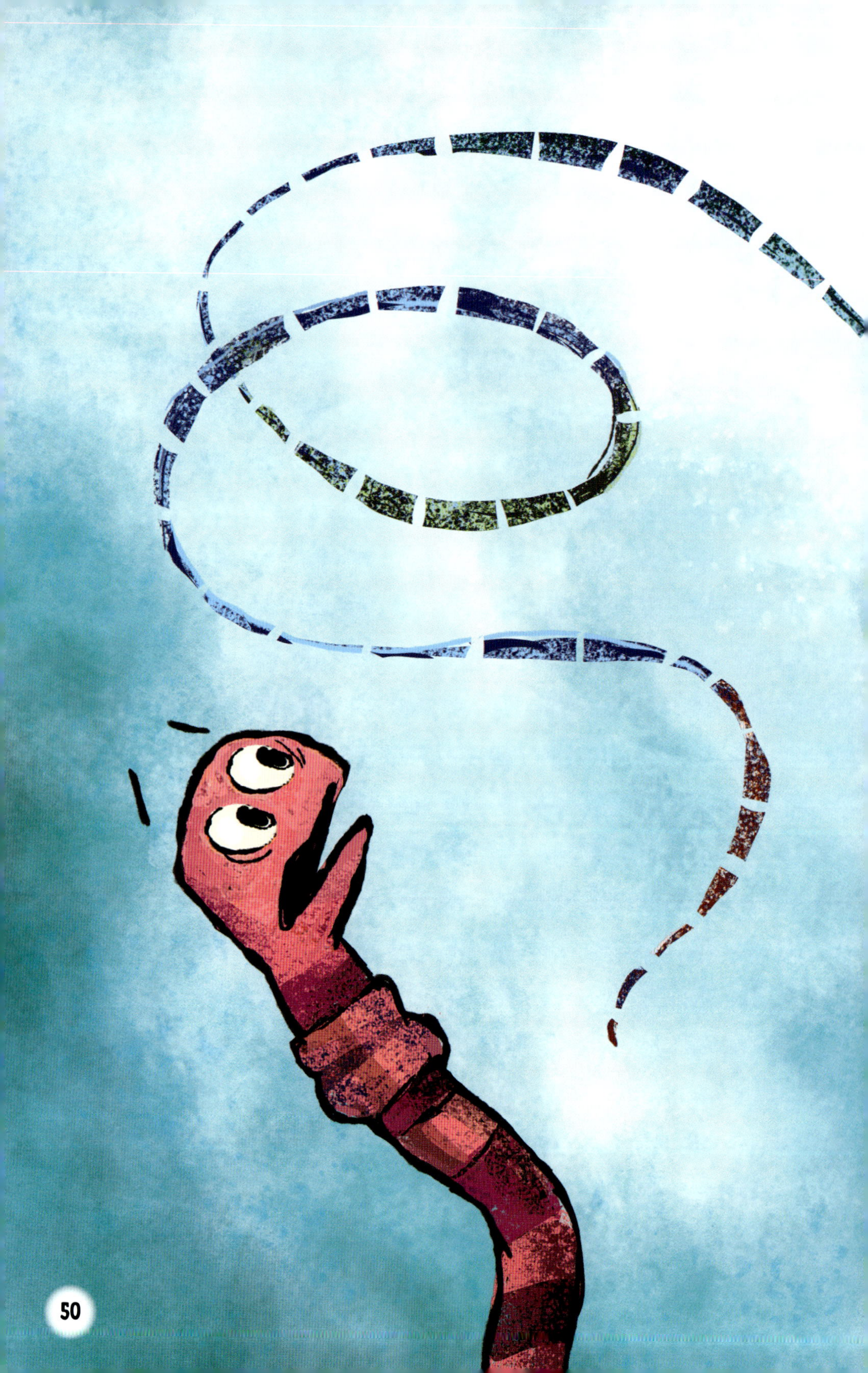

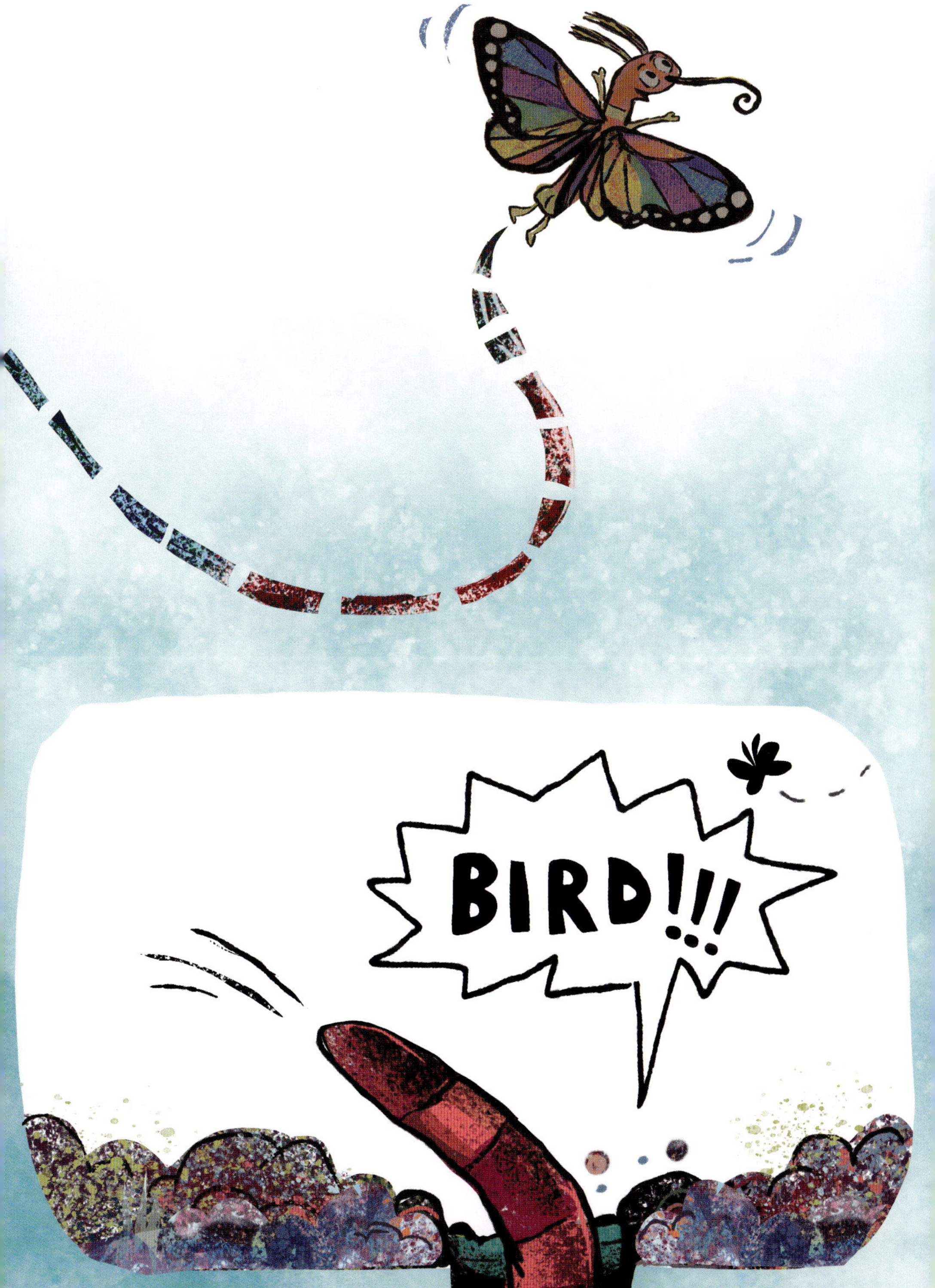
BIRD!!!

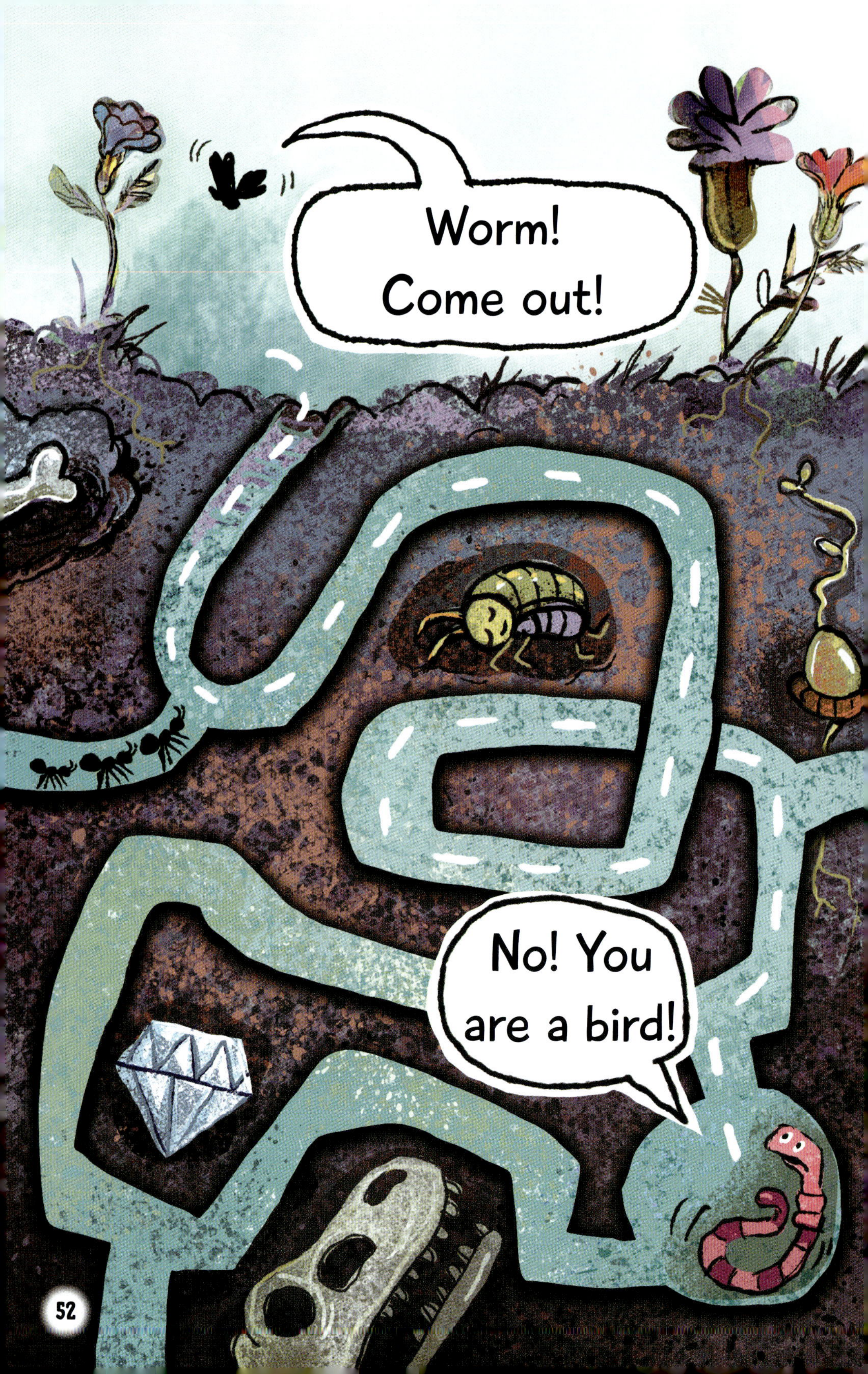
Worm!
Come out!
No! You
are a bird!

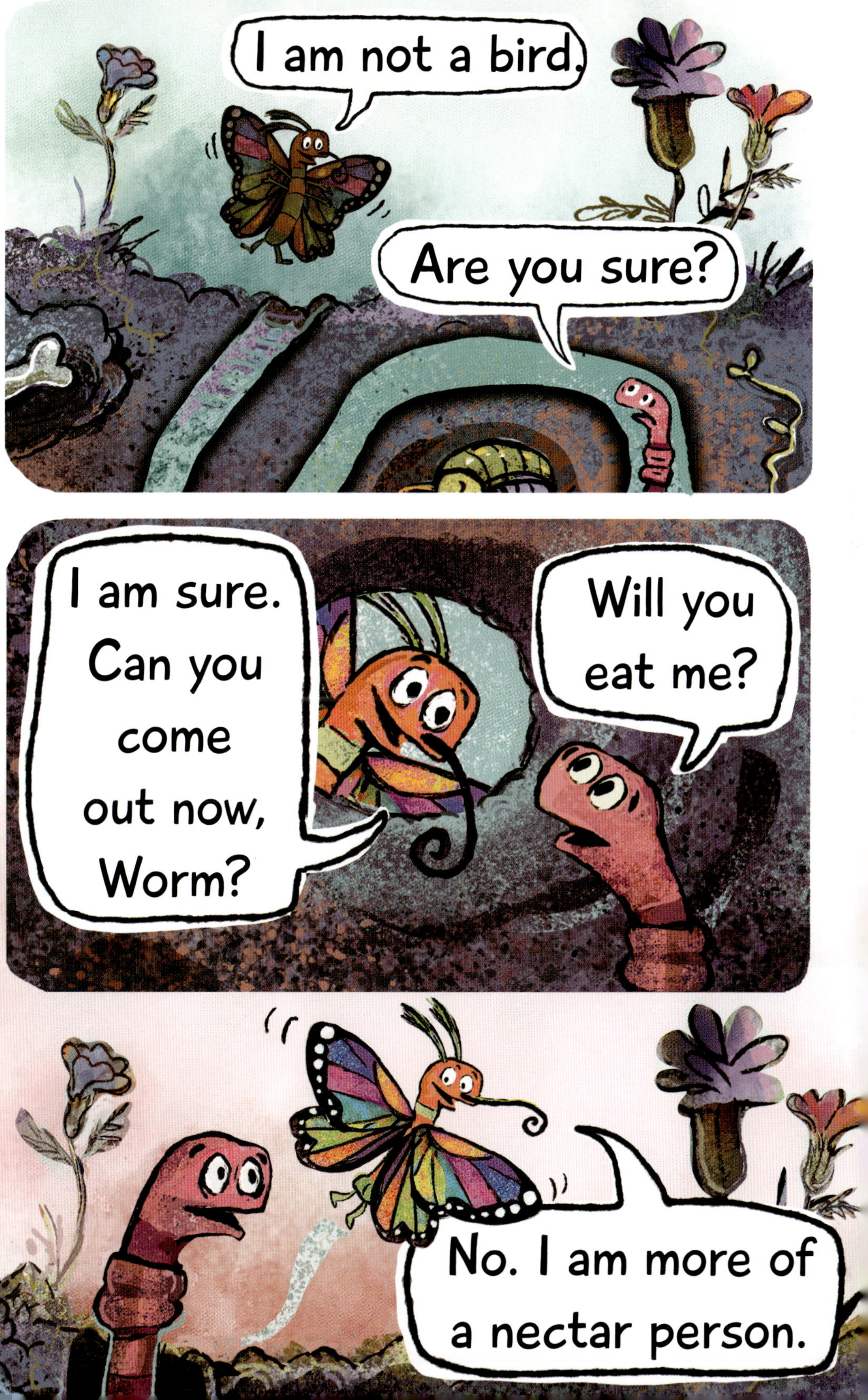
I am not a bird.
Are you sure?
I am sure. Can you come out now, Worm?
Will you eat me?
No. I am more of a nectar person.

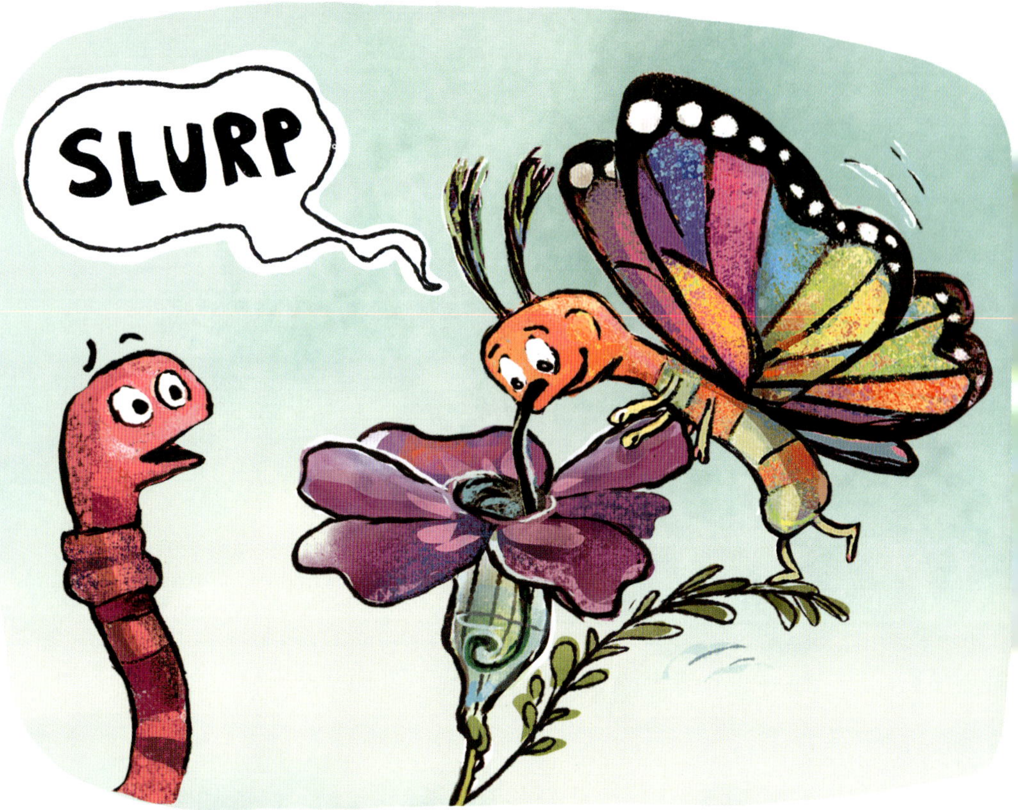
SLURP

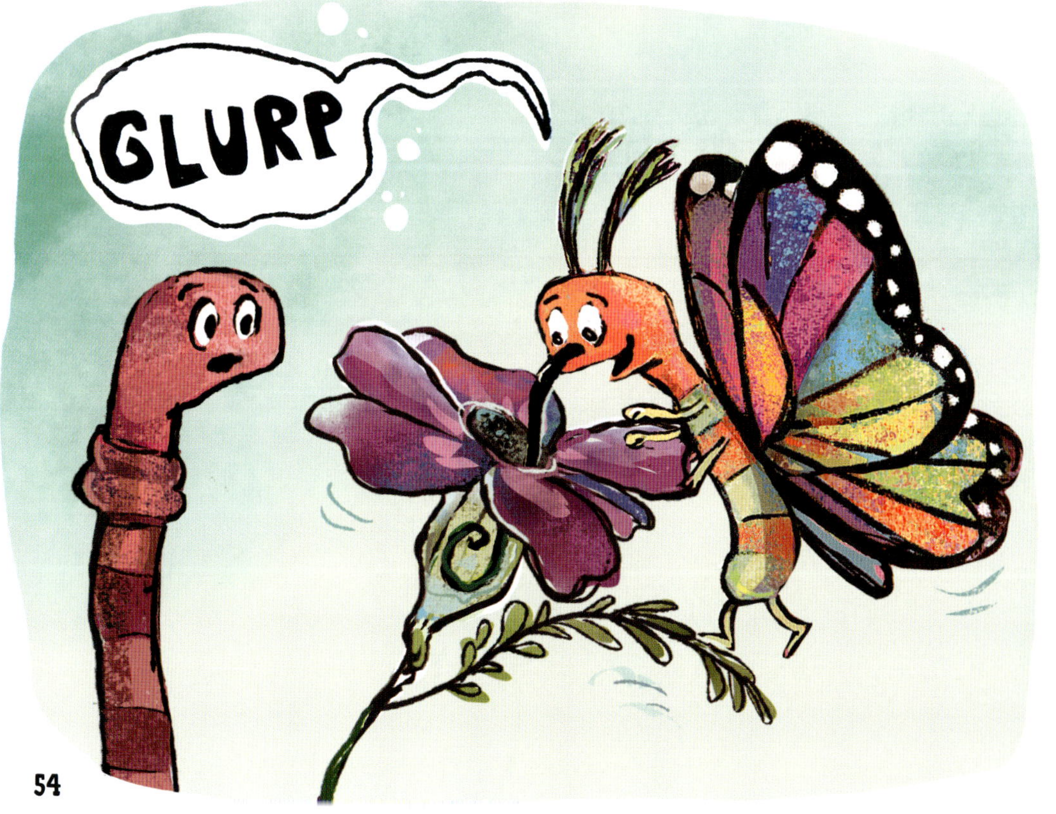
GLURP

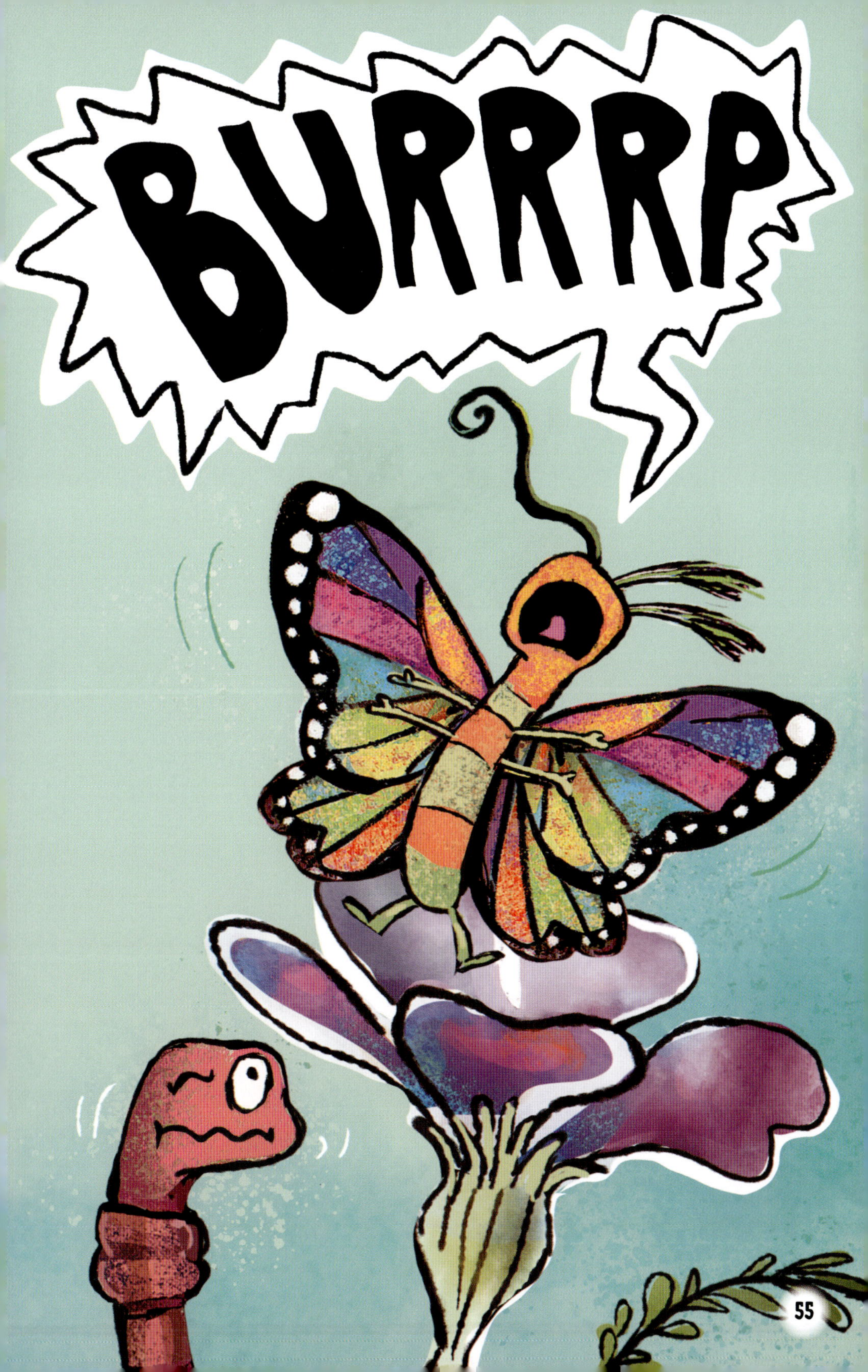
BURRRP

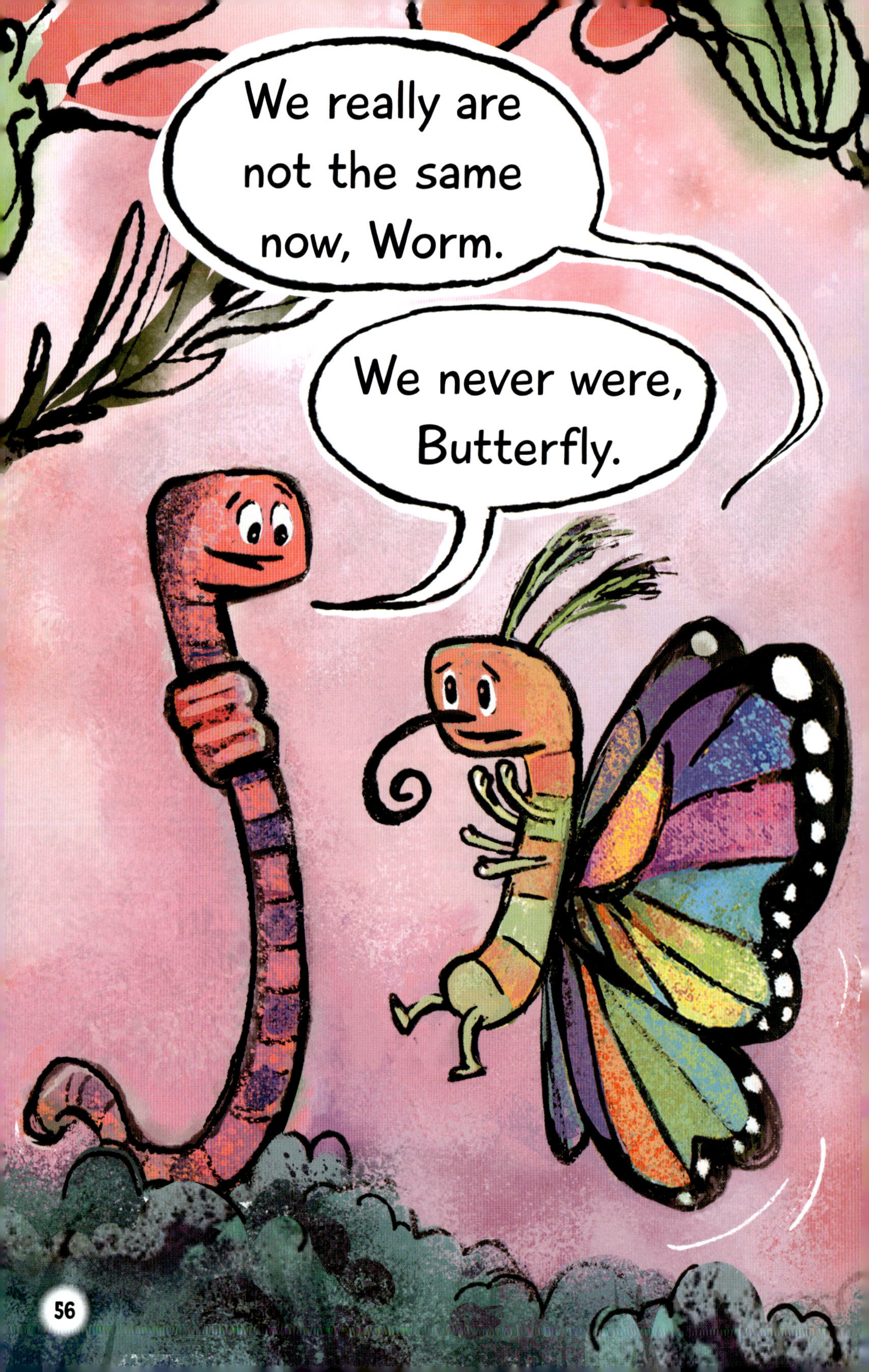
We really are not the same now, Worm.
We never were, Butterfly.

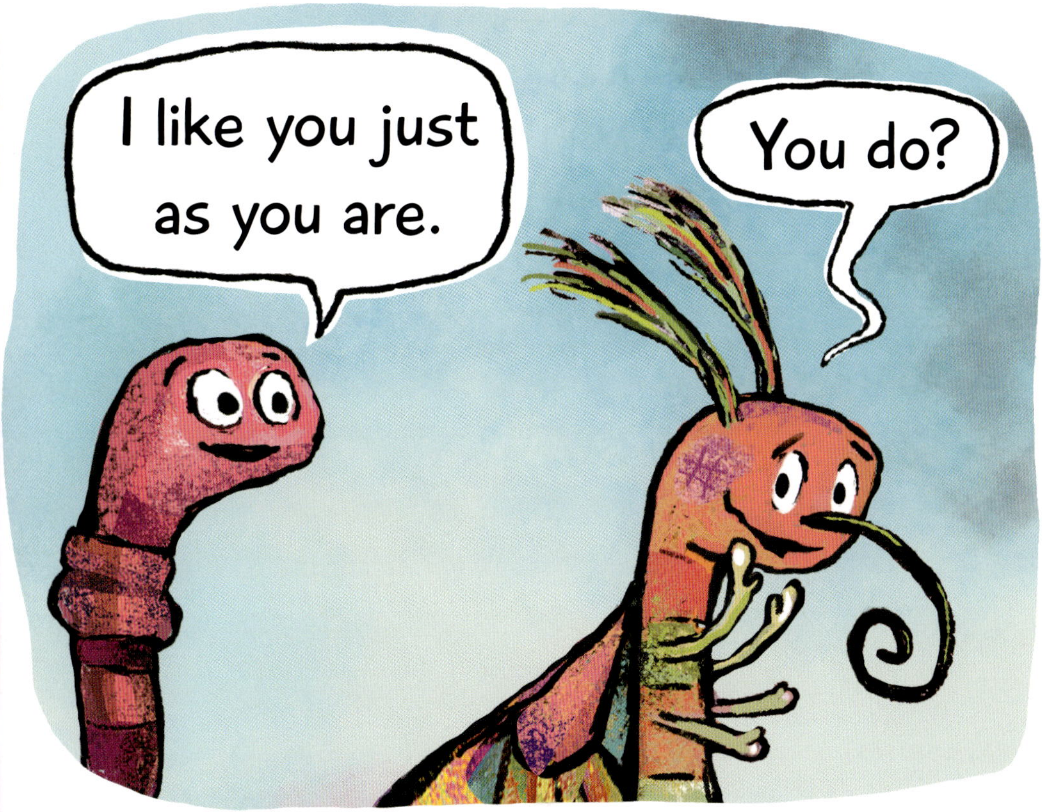
I like you just as you are.
You do?

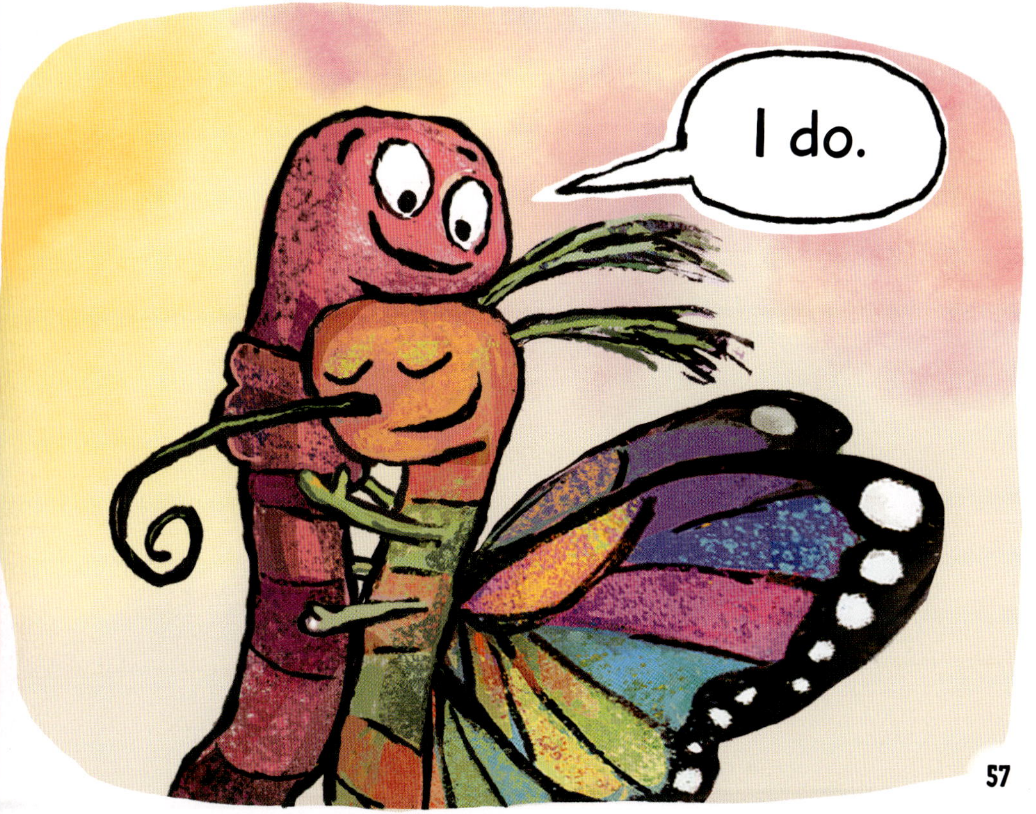
I do.

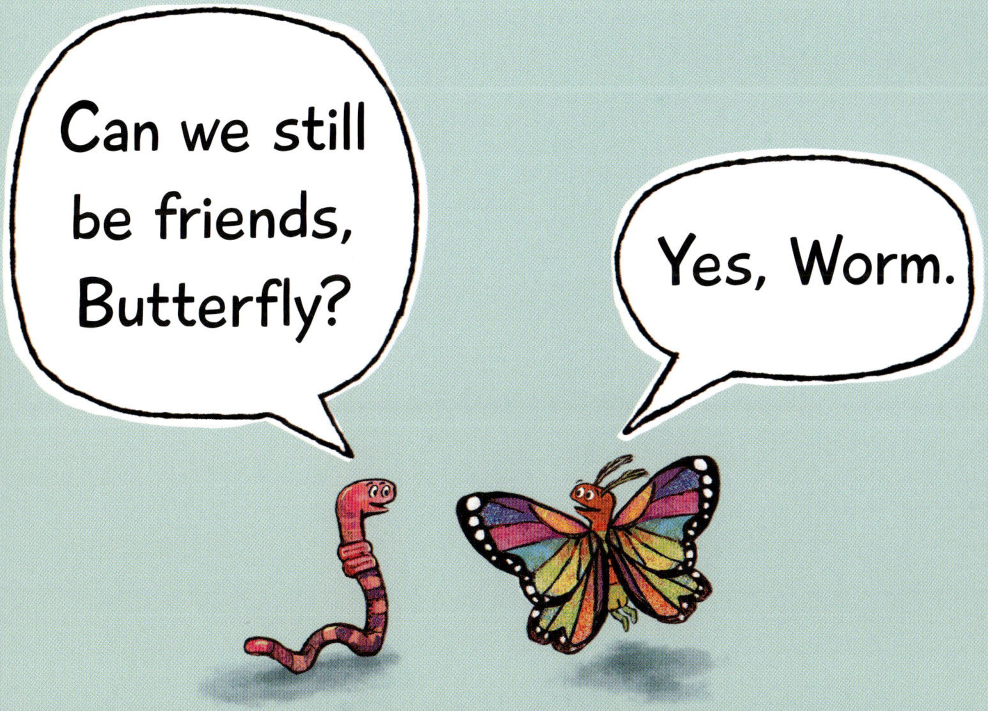
Can we still be friends, Butterfly?
Yes, Worm.

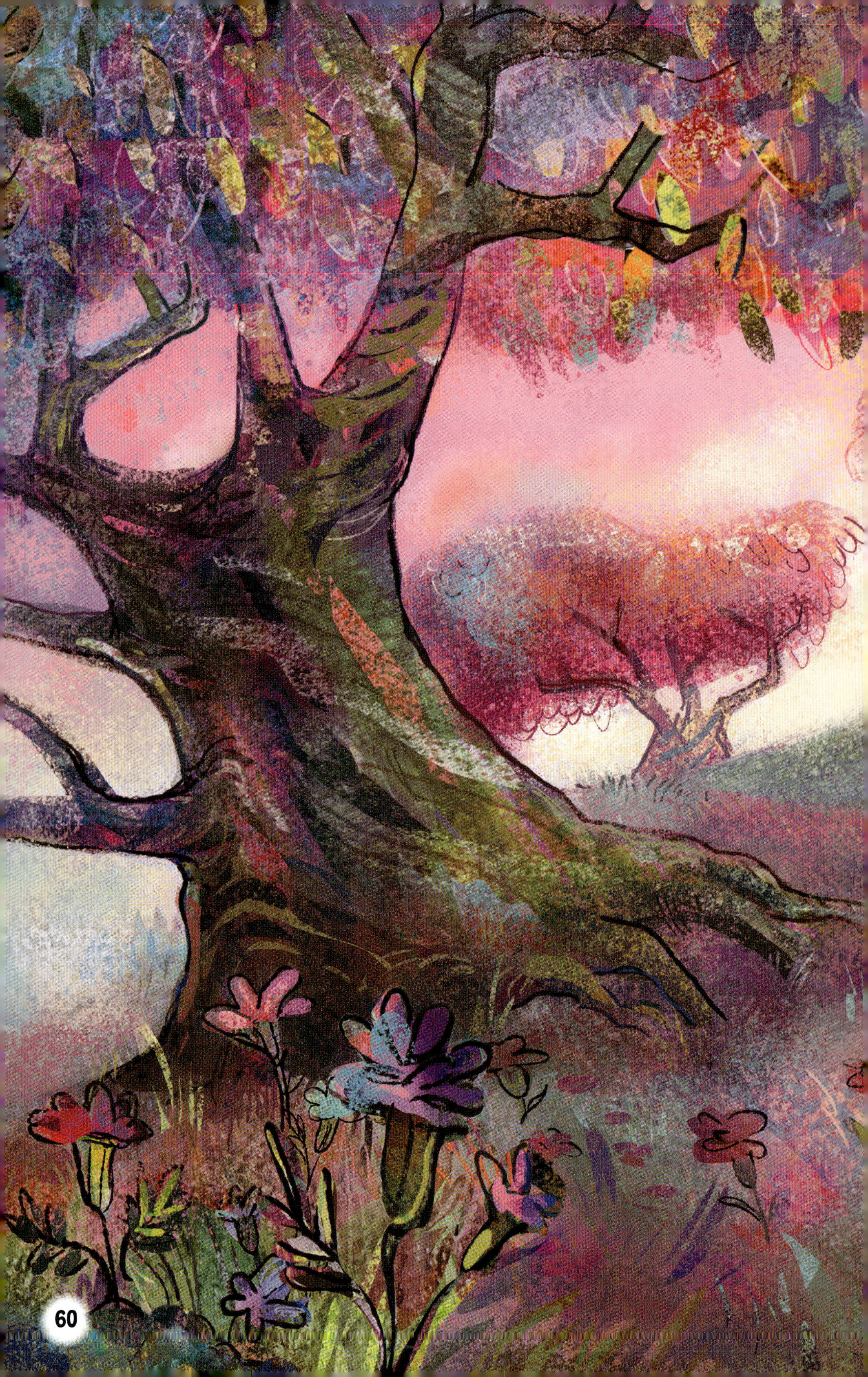

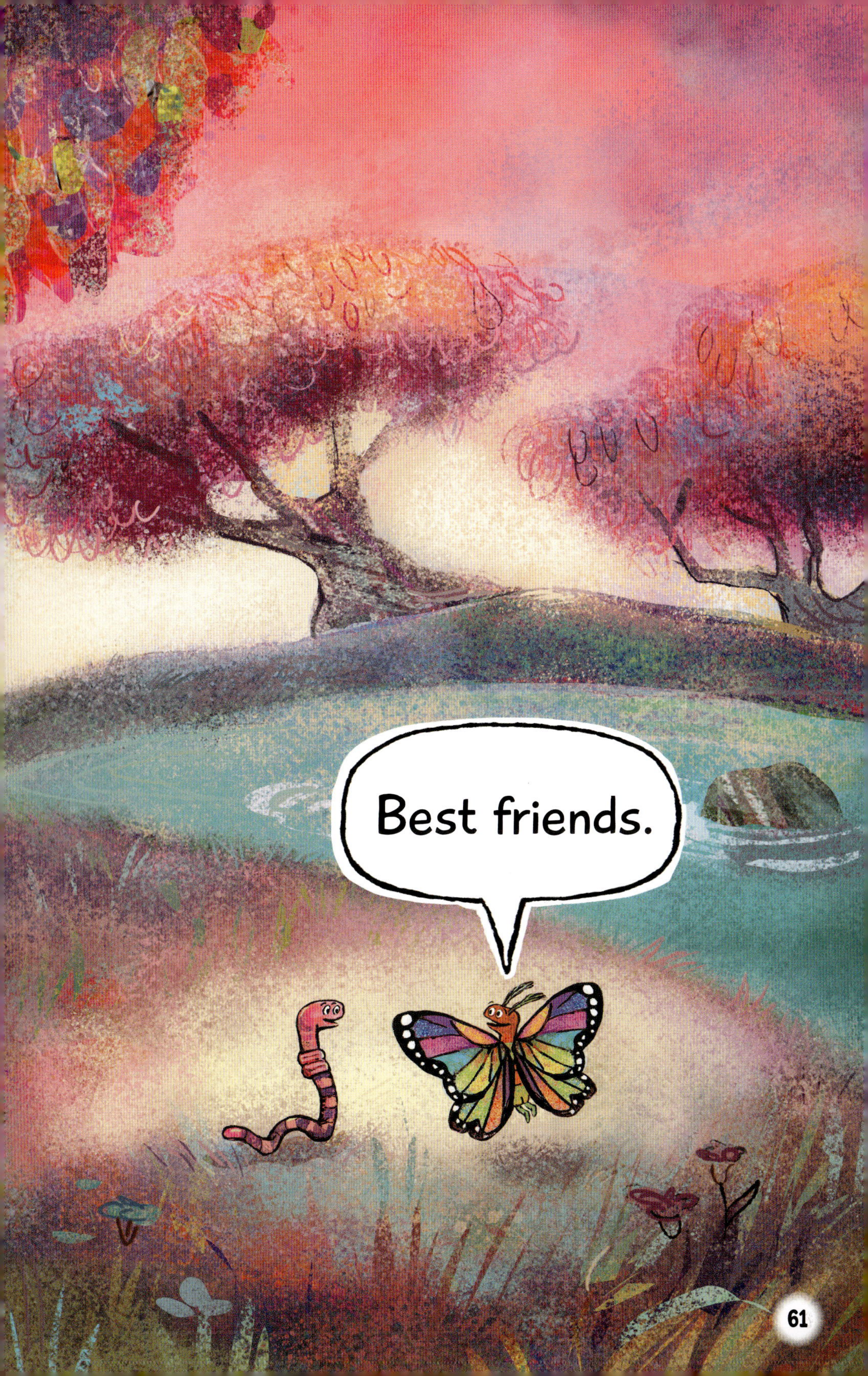
Best friends.

The life Cycle of a Worm

baby
cocoon
juvenile
(JOO-vuh-nile)
adult

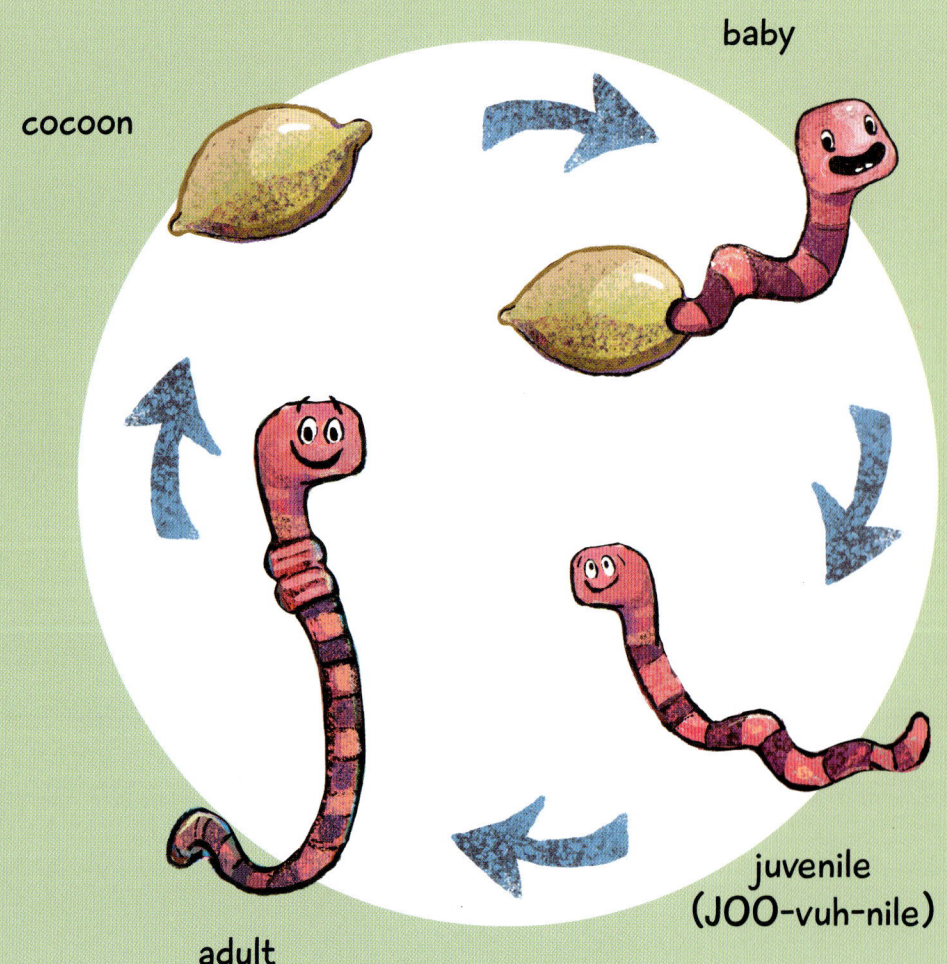

The life Cycle of a Butterfly

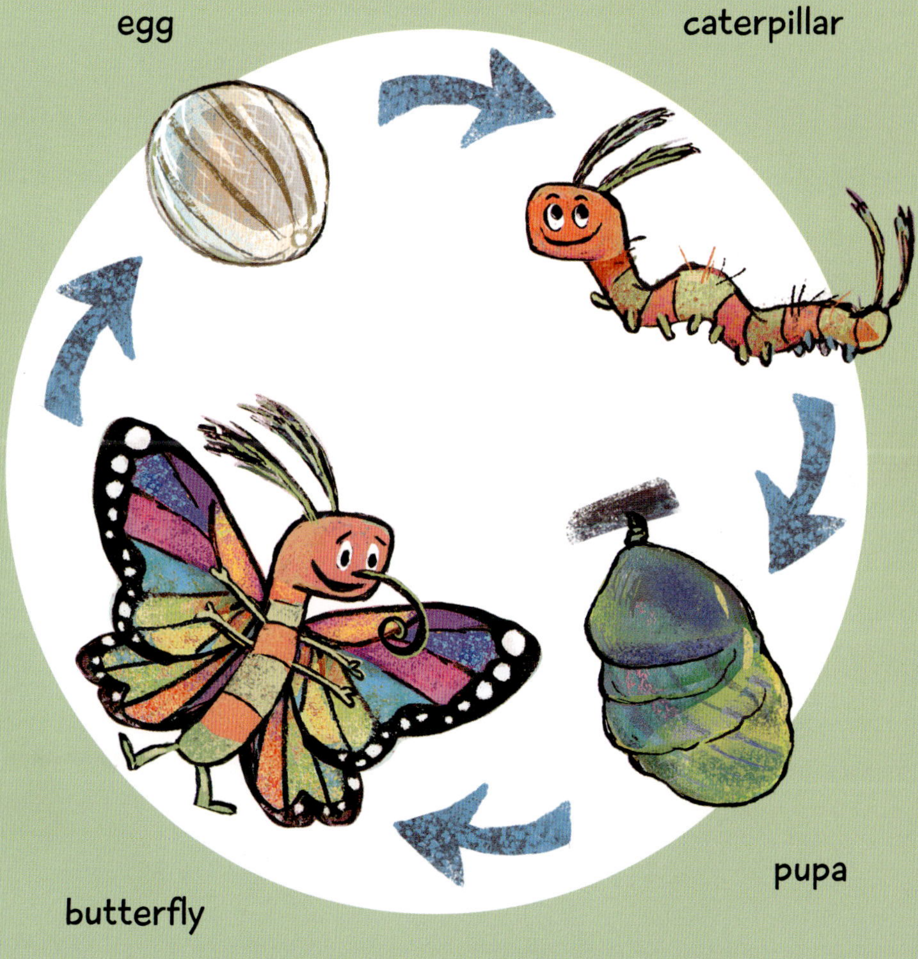
egg
caterpillar
pupa
butterfly

HOW TO DRAW WORM & BUTTERFLY

Worm

1. Draw a circle for the head, a square for the neck, and a rectangle for the body.

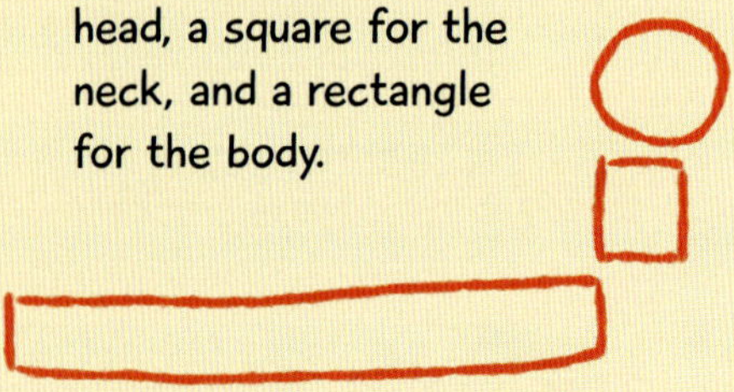

2. Connect the shapes with an outline.

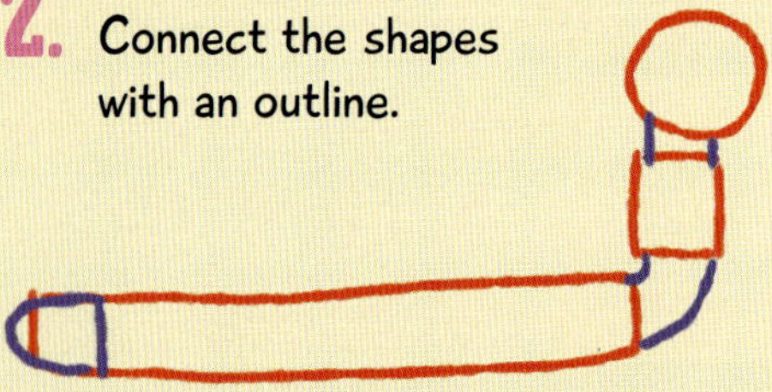

3. Draw lines for the body segments, dots for the eyes, and a triangle for the mouth.

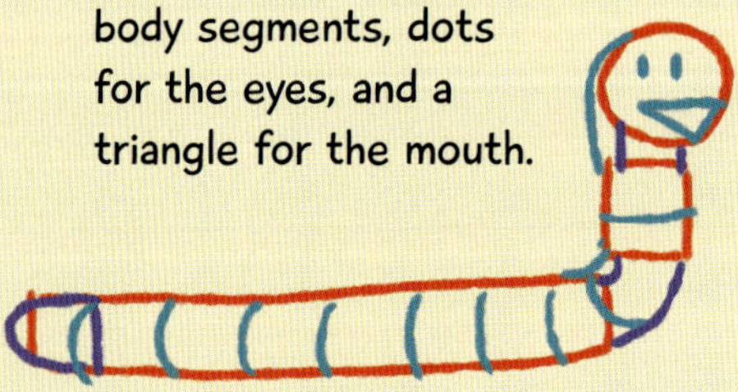

4. Clean up your drawing and erase any extra lines.

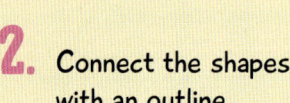
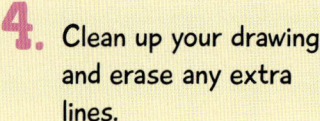

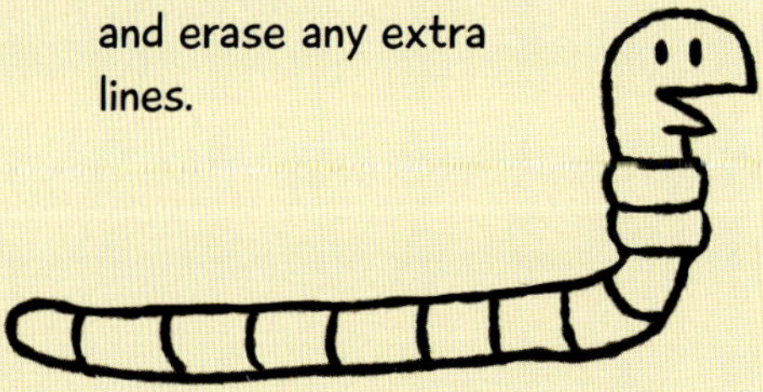

Butterfly

1. Draw a circle for the head, a rectangle for the body, and two hearts for the wings.

2. Connect the shapes with an outline. Add legs, a food tube, and tentacles.

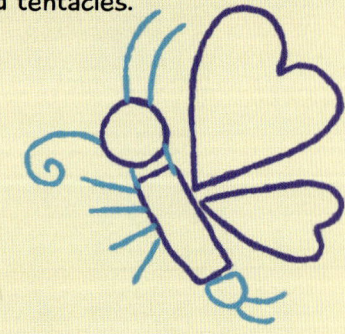

3. Draw a mouth and eyes, lines for the body segments, and veins and spots on the wings.